MW01133071

GOLD DIGGER

A BRIDGE TO ABINGDON NOVEL

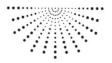

TATUM WEST

© 2019 Tatum West

All rights reserved. This book or any portion thereof may not be reproduced or used in any manner whatsoever without the express permission of the publisher except for the use of brief quotations in a book review.

This book is a work of fiction. Any resemblance to persons, living or dead, or places, events or locations is purely coincidental. The characters are all productions of the author's imagination.

Please note that this work is intended only for adults over the age of 18 and all characters represented are 18 or over.

Print Edition

Cover Design:
Mayhem Cover Creations

❧ Created with Vellum

PROLOGUE

GRAYSON

*S*ummer's over. All that's left are the lingering hot days of August. When the last of the tourists pack up and drive out, it leaves our little town alone to a crisp, lonesome autumn and bleak winter. Soon it will be cold, without the benefit of relief until spring comes again. When next spring arrives in Abingdon, Liam and I will both be long gone.

I glance through the twilight at him, taking in his angular, sculpted features for what may be the last time for a long time. When we were rising freshmen at Jackson Academy, I thought he was the most beautiful creature I'd ever beheld. In the four-odd years since then, I've come to realize Liam Gold is the most beautiful person on all of planet Earth. In that time, I've been lucky enough to make him my best friend. That took a lot of effort because honestly, no two people could be any more different than us.

I'm a math nerd without a lot of social skills, but a perfect score on the SAT. He's Jackson Academy's starting quarter-back, with an online fan club and an agent waiting in the wings for when he goes pro, leaving his NCAA status behind in a quest for the big money. In a million years, no one would have guessed we'd be friends. In a million years, no one would have ever imagined Liam Gold lounging beside me, leaning against a driftwood log by the lakeside, his hand on my knee, peering across the water at an old house we've both come to admire.

"I bet the guy who owns that place is a lawyer or a judge," Liam speculates as we watch a shadow pass from one lighted window to another. "It's gotta be somebody rich like that because no one else could afford the light bill."

He's not wrong. I've done sketches of the place – drawings to scale – and by my estimation, the ceilings are fifteen feet high and there are at least thirty rooms. The house is constructed of brick with a terra cotta roof and a stone foundation. It really is a showpiece.

"Maybe after I win a Superbowl, or seven of them, I can come back and buy a place like that," Liam says, grinning sideways at me.

"Or that place itself," I tell him. "It's the best one on the lake."

He laughs. "If that place was mine, I'd rip out that shitty front porch addition and take it back to the covered portico that it had a hundred years ago. And I'd restore the docks with a righteous boathouse."

Liam has a half-dozen other modifications he'd make to the nicest, most expensive property on the lake, but they're all reasonable. Most of them would improve the place, returning it to what it was historically. The house we're lusting after, after all, is an important late 19th century property that's been neglected in recent years. In truth, it's a miracle it's survived at all.

Liam and I have renovated that old house in our minds so many times we can barely even see it as it stands now.

"Maybe one day we'll get the chance to do all that," I tell him.

There's so much more I want to tell him.

Tomorrow I'm boarding a plane that will take me to the West Coast and the California Institute of Technology – Caltech – where I'll get to spend the next few years studying computer science and software development. The day after tomorrow, Liam will board a Greyhound bus that will take him to Blacksburg, Virginia where he'll join the Virginia Tech football team.

There's so much I need to tell him before we go our separate ways. There are so many emotions I want to share with him.

"I wouldn't have made it through Sophomore year without you," I blurt out, my chest tightening with the release of words. Tears rise from deep in my gut. "You didn't have to be friends with someone like me. You made this place bearable."

Liam slides back on his palms, cutting his eyes at me that way he does, with that sexy, knowing smile.

"That goes both ways," he says, his tone as smooth as warm honey. "You got me through calculus and chemistry with solid Bs. Without that, there would have been no scholarship to Virginia Tech."

He's got a point. It took a lot of work on my part to get his grades up, but he did his part too.

"We're both getting the hell out of this place," he says, trying to sound reassuring. "With any luck, we'll never come back again for anything except funerals. When we come back, all the papers will make note of it like it's a big deal."

I have no doubt that in Liam's case it will be a big deal. He's going to be a star athlete. He's going to be famous.

The sun has gone down and the air is taking on the first hint of autumn chill. I have a plane to catch early, so I go ahead with my bold move: throwing my arms around Liam, hugging him tight.

"When you're all rich and famous, don't forget me," I beg him, hoping, pulling him close. "Come home for spring break or Christmas, and let's get together. I swear I won't crowd you. I won't cramp your style."

"Like you ever could," Liam replies. Returning my hug, he slides his strong arms over my shoulders, pulling me tight to his chest. "Like I'd ever forget you. You're my bestie."

We stand like that a long time, trying to make the moment last, but soon we have to let go and admit to ourselves the moment has passed.

"I'll see you at spring break," he says, his breath warm against my neck. "Or next summer. Or sometime."

"Text me," I say. "If you want to." My heart sticks in my throat. I will the tears not to choke me. I feel like we're breaking up – which is stupid – because we've never been anything more than just friends. We've both been too scared to take it any further.

"You're gonna make a whole slew of new friends – guys who are a lot smarter than me – out in California," Liam says, pulling away, taking a step back. It's dark so I can't see him well, but I swear he has a catch in his voice. "You don't need me hitting your phone up from back here in the sticks. If you're around this summer, look me up."

"Ah… okay," I respond, hesitating, trying to catch his drift and not sound needy. "Yeah, and you're gonna be slammed with games and practice and training. Yeah. This summer we'll catch up."

"Yeah," Liam repeats, nodding vigorously, turning away from me. "Have a great year at Caltech. Don't study too hard. Enjoy California at least a little for me."

"I will," I say, following his lead, moving to our cars parked nearby. "I promise."

He gets in his car and I get in mine. We start our engines and both pull out at the same time. Liam takes a left and I take a right. I drive slowly, watching his tail lights grow smaller and smaller in my rearview mirror until they disappear behind a curve in the dark. When they flicker out of view, I realize that I've never felt more alone in my entire life.

***

The summer after my freshman year, I came home looking for Liam. I learned he wasn't coming back to Abingdon at all because he had a football camp in Maine. The following year, he was in London prepping for an exhibition game. The year after that, he was on the Olympic Team practicing in Beijing.

Four years after our last night on the lake, I was a senior at Caltech running an already money-making tech startup out of my dorm suite. Liam was in his senior year at Virginia Tech. He was the starting quarterback on the top college team in the nation that year; the Cavaliers were on fire and Liam was the hottest flame on the field. It was a Sunday afternoon in mid-December when I did something so out of character that almost everyone in my dorm thought I might be ill. I stopped working and I went out to the common area to watch football on television.

The Virginia Tech team faced off against Iowa in a game that would determine who played for the national championship title. They were the number one and number three ranked teams in the country, respectively. The showdown had been promoted to death, and Liam was already a top draft pick. Watching him play in that game alongside my rowdy neighbors, I knew by the following year – barring catastrophe – he was going to be pulling in seven figures.

I'll never forget the moment it happened. Someone passed me a box with a few slices of greasy pizza remaining in it, the saturated crust congealed to a glue-like substance stuck fast to the cardboard. I looked down at the unappetizing slices, then glanced up at the television screen just in time to see Liam sacked by a big guy who seemed as surprised by the hit as I was.

Liam went down and everyone in the room let out a collective "Aghhhh!" as if they'd taken the hit themselves. A few of them cursed, searing their eyes closed against the horrific image on the high definition screen.

At first, I don't understand what happened.

"Yo! Ellis! You know Liam Gold, don't you?" A guy from the front calls out, looking back at me from his comfortable spot on the overstuffed couch. He uses my last name to address me like we're *compadres* on the soccer team.

All eyes in the room turn to me. I nod.

"He's done," the guy says with a smirk. "That was epic! Hope he was insured. Joe Theismann got two million dollars when that happened to him."

There was blood and a lot of sick looking coaches and trainers on the field. Most of them worked to get Liam secured on a backboard for transport before they could resume the game. Never having watched a football game before, I thought – erroneously – this was just what happened when someone got tackled. I didn't comprehend what "He's done" actually meant.

It meant he was done. *Really done*. His football career was over. He would never earn so much as a nickel from it, despite helping the team earn millions in television revenues while he played and leading the team to victory in one championship season after another.

During those four years of college, Liam and I never managed to get together. After his injury, when I was home on spring break, I went to see him in the hospital. I was told he was in physical therapy. I came back a few days later and got a different story. A few days after that, they started recycling the excuses. I realized Liam didn't want to see me. As confusing and hurtful as that was, I also understood. Liam didn't want to be seen weak and broken, not even to me.

Growing up, Liam was always my strong man. He was my buffer against the bullies. He was my best friend and my sounding board when I came out to my parents, who freaked and said I was going to grow up to be a disco diva drag queen. He solved my problems and made space for me to grow into the person I always had the potential to be. His friendship infused me with confidence. Liam's the reason I had guts enough to take every risk I've ever taken. He's the man who made it possible for me to be who I am today.

Yet, at the time, all I knew is that for four years while we were in college, we never managed to get our schedules together. He was an important, successful, famous athlete. I was just a geeky college kid ten states away. Liam never needed me, and I couldn't fathom a world where he might. I was capable of imagining all kinds of software and tech products that defied physics and confounded science, but the idea of Liam Gold needing anything I might have to offer? That idea was alien to me.

This is the story of how that all changed.

CHAPTER ONE

GRAYSON - SEVEN YEARS LATER

*A*bingdon's main drag writhes like a sea flowing with people. The streets are blocked off on both ends of town, and every corner boasts a performer with a bucket for change situated front and center before the crowd.

When I was a kid growing up here, Buskerfest was not this big of a deal. There might be a few bands playing covers and a fire eater or two, but there was nothing like this Vegas-level production. From perpetual motion machines crawling down the street, winding through the crowd under their own kinetic steam, to an entire circus acrobatic act vaulting from street lamp post to crosswalk and back again, this festival seems to have grown up and into an eclectic, slightly weird incarnation of its founding vision.

"Hurry up, Grayson," my sister Mel goads, pulling me along by my belt loops. "We're gonna be late."

Melanie, who usually goes by Mel, has always been punctual. She's also attractive with perfect manners, Princess Kate style, and an uncanny sense of just what people are up to. If she'd had a shred of ambition beyond simply marrying well, she would have made a damn fine police detective. As it stands, all she's qualified to do is point out to me and anyone else within earshot that I'm holding up the party. She's in a hurry and I'm straggling, taking in the scenery.

Back home in Mountain View where my company is located, I don't get a chance to get out much. When I'm not working (I'm *always* working) I'm sure as shit not out on the streets rubbing elbows with the riffraff. I have people who I pay to brave the world for me. They grocery shop and get my car serviced, pick up my dry cleaning, and fetch my takeout sushi when I give my chef the night off.

Here in Abingdon – where I grew up – I don't bring my chef with me. When visiting home, I'm slumming it — or *living authentically*, I guess you could say. It makes me appreciate what I've accomplished so far in life—the ability to outsource.

A man on stilts standing at least eighteen feet tall ambles by, doffing his hat in my direction with a wink. He's attractive if you can excuse his height and his profession. I never was attracted to artists. Not that kind anyway. That said, I'm not sure when I've ever been surrounded by so damn many fantastic looking, shirtless men. Buskerfest is – as far as I can discern – a mostly topless event. And very *gay*. Just the way I like it.

Maybe there are so many bare chests because it's still damn near ninety-five degrees even though the sun slipped beneath the horizon an hour ago. This may be one of those nights that doesn't ever cool off. Either way, I'm enjoying the show.

We're headed to a puppet show. I'm not talking about sock puppets either. These puppets are massive, complicated, and in some cases take two or three people to operate. They don't look like puppets. They look like authentic dragons, megalodons, and fantastic, prehistoric feathered birds. There are also flat-footed giants pulled straight from the solid text of a snowy George R.R. Martin novel.

We get there just in time to see a trio of scarlet red Satyrs buck violently, raring back on hind legs, then settle down into a dance routine to the music of the Eagles' *Witchy Woman*; the seething drumbeat is a perfect platform for three mythical creatures dancing on cloven hooves.

Mel and her fiancé, Dexter, are into the show, but this isn't exactly my scene.

"I'll be back in a few minutes," I shout in Mel's ear, trying to be heard over the music. "I'm going to see if I can find Elias."

I know Elias Spaulding, a fellow high-tech entrepreneur, is here with his famous artist husband, Zane Chase. They're way more my speed than my sister and her mostly-psycho fiancé, who both need to be down in the guts of the crowd to see every act do its thing. Me, I prefer a slightly elevated platform from which to observe the goings on.

I locate Elias's VIP tent, which is already packed with Abingdon's A-list crowd. Nikki Rippon, a once-upon-a-time rockstar, who's more recently a local arts scene mover and shaker and his dashing husband Fox (who I heard was a Hollywood lawyer, but now he's the county Sheriff) hold court near the open bar. I could sidle up next to them and spend the rest of the night basking in the warm smiles and sweet graces of them and their hangers on, or...

What. The. Fuck?

A dozen paces outside the security perimeter, I spy six-feet, three-inches of the finest specimen of long-lost human masculinity I've seen this decade. He passes by my periphery, causing my head to swing around so fast I might need a chiropractic adjustment.

It's him.

He breezes on, sightless, not even paying attention as he

floats so far outside our reality. He's got a plastic bag in one hand and a long pole in the other, with a big roan-colored dog on his heel, sticking close by.

I side-step out of the security line, dropping into the crowd.

"Liam?" My throat goes hoarse, and something inside of me starts to break.

The sound of his name sticks on my tongue as it sticks in the air. It's been so long since I spoke the word out loud.

"Liam?"

He stops, brow furrowed, looking up. He gazes past me, then realizing I'm the one speaking, settles on me with all his inquiry.

"Liam," I say. "Dude, where have you been?"

I've looked everywhere, even hiring a private investigator to track his social security number. Nothing has turned up for at least two years. He's gone completely off-grid.

He blinks, hearing my voice, trying to reconcile it with the figure standing before him.

"Grayson?" he asks, his voice loaded with doubt.

I nod. I'm not as tall as he is, but I'm not too far off. I'm almost as big as he is thanks to my personal trainer and a shit-ton of time spent in the gym. That said, I think he's lost some bulk since his college football days.

"Yeah," I reply. "It's me. Jesus, son. Where the fuck have you been?"

I have no ability to contain my delight at finding Liam after all these years. My arms fly around his shoulders and I hug him – *tight*. The dog at his side stands up straight, its back arching, hair standing up on end oddly, its eyes narrowing. He finally decides I'm good people, snuggling against my leg, offering a paw as Liam and I reconnect, giddy with our reunion.

"Here and there," he says, laughing. "Around. Man, you

look great. All grown up. Last I saw you, you were a hundred twenty pounds soaking wet with peach fuzz tickling your lip. Look at you. You're almost as big as me. Amazing."

"Yeah, man. I've been working on it." I grin. Our eyes lock for a moment, and I feel the electricity in the air grow thick and hot.

He's right. I was a late bloomer, along with being a full two years younger than most of the kids in our class because I skipped two grades. I graduated high school at sixteen years old. Liam was a year older than everyone else because he failed fourth grade. (He got mono and never learned his multiplication tables). Missing something like that can screw you up for life. In his case, it almost did, except we became friends, and I worked him through it. When we graduated high school, I was sixteen, and he was almost nineteen.

So much has happened since then. We need to catch each other up. I could tell him I saw the hit that ended his football career. I could tell him that I've tried for years to find him. I could tell him there's never been anyone who stuck in my head or stuck through my heart the way he did.

"Liam, let's go get a drink. I'm buying," I say. The things I really want to catch up on have less to do with talking than they do with reacquainting ourselves in a more intimate way, but I'll take what I can get.

He looks at me, then down at his dog, then back up at me. "I... I..." he says. "I'd love that, but I can't leave Beau..."

"Bring him," I say. "We'll go back to my place. He's welcome."

I drive my Audi rental with Beau the dog loitering between the seats in a state of moderate anxiety. He's an odd canine. He's got intelligent, expressive eyes, a muscular build, and an oddly patterned growth of shiny fur spiking down his spine, like someone groomed him badly

"He's okay," Liam assures me. "Just not used to the car.

13

He's used to my truck. He doesn't much like driving at all. He was in a car wreck. That's how I got him."

"A wreck?" I ask, reaching across the console to stroke the animal's big head. "Did he get hit?"

Liam shakes his head, looking away from me, out the window. "No," he says. "There was a big wreck out on the highway a few years back. A pileup in the rain. I found Beau the day after, walking along the side of the highway looking for something. His paws were shredded with broken glass and he was all bruised and torn up, still wearing his seat harness and tags from South Africa."

"South Africa?"

He nods. "There was a couple killed in the accident. They were from South Africa, vacationing here. They brought their dog with them. He's a purebred Rhodesian Ridgeback. It said so on the customs forms they had to fill out for the flight over. I never could find out what they named him, so I named him Beau."

That's an amazing story, and no less amazing that Liam came across him.

"He's lucky you found him," I say. "He might have been wandering out there for months, or worse, gotten hit, if you hadn't discovered him."

"I'm the lucky one," Liam says, his tone sounding far away. "Beau's been the best friend I could ever hope for. More than I deserve."

Once upon a time I was Liam's best friend, but that was before football scholarships and technology companies. We were kids. The idea that I'm so easily replaced by a dog, however, smarts more than I care to admit. I expected Liam would have followed the path of Elias Spaulding or Nikki Rippon and found some significant other who completed him. I wonder why he never did.

"So, what brings you back to town?" Liam asks, posing the first question he's asked so far.

I realize then I've been asking all the questions, and he's been giving vague non-answers.

"My sister's getting married," I respond. "I'm here for her engagement party, and to assure our parents that she's not marrying a serial killer. They don't much like him."

Liam laughs, surprising himself. His laugh – the smile that comes with it – is disarming and charming and sexy as hell. It's unchanged since ninth grade when I first fell in love with it.

"Seriously?" he asks. "Your sister's perfect. Always has been. How could they not like her fiancé? What's wrong with him?"

I shrug. "No one's good enough for Mel," I say. "She's their princess. They think he's marrying her country club membership. He may be, for all I know. It's not really any of my business. I think she loves him, despite the fact that he's a little odd. He treats her well and he has a good job. It could be worse."

Liam nods, falling silent. I watch his hand move up to cover the frayed patch of fabric near the knee of his jeans. His clothes are well-worn and dingy. He needs a haircut. His nails are ragged and dirty. There's a hollow gauntness in his cheeks that I've seen before in the hard men who live in the Tenderloin neighborhood of San Francisco. If he's not living rough, he's not far from it. I'm surprised I didn't notice before, but I was so excited just to see him again.

"I haven't had anything to eat all night," I say, turning off toward the lake. "I'll order us an extra-large pizza as soon as we get home. Decide what you want on it."

Liam plays it very cool, but I can hear his stomach growl. Just the mention of a meal sends his digestive tract into spasms.

I'll feed him caviar and avocado on toast, with steaks of smoked salmon smeared with cream cheese if he'll hang around with me. Liam Gold isn't going hungry on my watch.

"Where are we going?" he asks, his tone rising. "You're headed toward the lake."

"My place in Abingdon," I remind him, grinning. "You'll see. I bet you like it."

Liam's eyes grow wide with wonder and surprise as soon as we clear the cover of trees. He recognizes it. How could he not? We stared at it for hours on end as kids, imagining all manner of stories we'd live out between its walls, under its many-gabled, slate roof.

"You own this?" Liam asks, his voice shrinking.

I nod. "Yeah," I say. "I bought it late last year."

I bought it the second it was listed for sale. I've had a realtor in town watching it forever. My plan is to completely rehabilitate it, but I just haven't gotten around to it yet. I put a new roof on and updated the master bath and the kitchen so they were usable, but other than that, I've done next to nothing to it. It needs a lot of work. It needs a loving touch to do it right. I figure I'll be here more once Mel is married. Even if I'm not—I wanted this place, and I have more than enough money to keep it up.

Liam blinks, shaking his head. He stays silent as we come inside, just taking in the place for the first time.

I lead him through a series of mostly empty, but still beautiful, rooms toward the kitchen where there's both refreshment and furniture. As we pass through the old formal dining room, Liam's calloused hands linger on the wainscoting, his index finger caressing the contours of the finely detailed molding like a lover might caress a hip bone or breast.

"Walnut," he whispers under his breath. "Gorgeous."

When we were kids, Liam used to speculate about the

16

woodwork in this house. From the parquet floors in the ballroom to the exquisite cabinetry in the butler's pantry just off the kitchen, he knew his wood even then. I remember he worked as a carpenter with one of his uncles during the summer months. He was a good carpenter as I recall it, and he enjoyed the work.

The private investigator I hired noted that Liam made a living as a carpenter not long after leaving the rehab facility where he recuperated following the surgeries to repair his leg. Then that work stopped with no explanation. The PI postulated a drug problem or something similar. I always doubted that idea. Liam was too smart, too grounded, to be involved in something so self-destructive.

"You used to do carpentry," I observe, going to the bar, pouring two neat Islay Scotches. "Do you still?"

Liam shakes his head, then calls Beau to heel beside him. The dog sniffs around, finding the place fascinating.

"No," he says. "All my tools got stolen. I couldn't replace them, so… I don't do carpentry anymore."

I hand Liam his drink, sizing him up. He's not lying to me. He's just stating a fact.

"I'm gonna go order that pizza," I say. "Make yourself at home."

I kick my shoes off in the hallway on the way to finding the phone number for Abingdon's best delivered pizza. (It's a short list).

While talking to the pizza guy, I'm intellectually multitasking, wondering exactly how many slices of pizza and drinks consumed is enough before I can make a move and put Liam in my bed. His body heat from the next room is just about enough to send me into palpitations. In high school we fooled around tentatively, but that was it. I don't think a day has passed since graduation that I haven't regretted that fact.

Maybe I'm getting a do over.

17

Coming back into the dining room where I left Liam and Beau, I find the dog sitting quietly beside his master, who stands at the big picture window overlooking the sprawling yard and the wide expanse of lake beyond it. He peers through the darkness across the lake toward the spot he and I used to haunt as boys.

"I reckon kids still camp out over there, staring at this place, fantasizing about it," I say, coming up alongside him to share the view.

Liam nods, crossing his arms over his chest. "Yeah," he acknowledges, his tone leaden with melancholy. He doesn't break his gaze or turn my way. "The big difference is you made your fantasies come true."

Not all of them, I muse to myself. If he only knew the fantasies I've kept close all these years. If he only knew how I wish I'd acted on those impulses so long ago. I was too afraid to take a risk.

Am I still afraid? Time will tell.

Other than his observation about dreams come true, Liam is a man of precious few words. He loses himself in devouring the pizza as soon as it arrives, swallowing big chewy chunks of crust almost whole while swigging gulp after gulp of frothy IPA. For some reason, watching him eat and drink with enthusiasm makes me happy. I derive a sense of personal accomplishment from it that I don't deserve, but do enjoy.

Just watching him sit at my table makes me smile.

Liam looks up from his empty plate, a few moist crumbs sticking to his stubbled chin. He blinks.

"What?" he asks, caught like a deer in the headlights.

I shake my head. "Just you," I tell him. "You're so stunningly beautiful, it takes my breath."

I reach up to his chin and with two fingers and brush the pizza crumbs away. My fingers linger, tracing his jawline, feeling the sharp stubble of several days' growth shadowing his skin.

Liam stiffens as if he's surprised by my touch. His hand rises to meet mine, fingers circling. He closes his eyes, exhaling anxiously, as if my touch causes him some small, exquisite pain.

"I want to kiss you," I tell him. "I don't want to stop there."

Liam's eyes open. His grey irises have gone dark, shadowed with something unspoken. His full, plump lips flatten as if he's afraid to speak, as if words have failed him.

"Probably… not…. a good… idea," he stutters, his hand still wrapped around mine, his breath caught in his throat.

Bullshit.

I lean forward, lifting my free hand toward him, circling his head at the back of his neck, pulling him close into a kiss. His lips are cool and sweet and, despite his doubts, he meets my kiss and returns it with a hunger and heat that speak louder than his words.

I've wanted Liam Gold's lips on mine since the first time I ever laid eyes on him, back when we were both jailbait and clueless. I've imagined this moment a thousand times. I never thought I'd get the opportunity to bring it to life. Once before I let him slip away, but not this time. This time I'm doing things the right way.

"Let's take this upstairs," I whisper, my lips grazing his ear, my breath hot on his skin. "I'll prove it's a *very good* idea."

Liam literally shudders, trembling under my touch. His breath comes fast and hard.

"I want too, Gray. More than you know."

"I won't pressure you," I say. "But I can show you a very, very good time." I'm already hard, cock pulsing, my body lit from within with the fiery need I've kept inside of me for so many years.

Beau rises with us to follow, but Liam stops him in his

tracks, telling him to sit, then lie down. "I'll be back," he says to the chastened animal. "Stay."

At the foot of the stairs Liam slows, looking up at me with an expression I can't fathom.

"I need…" he starts, taking one step at a time, moving slowly, methodically, as if it's painful.

I remember his injury and the shattered knee. Liam used to move with such graceful alacrity, but given what happened, it's understandable that the steps are a challenge. I slow my pace.

"I need to take a shower," he says, finishing his thought before we reach the top of the steps.

Not a problem. I grin at him, pulling him along. "We can accommodate that," I reply. "I like to play in the water."

Liam shakes his head. "No," he states. "I *really* need a shower. A long hot one. *Alone*."

He holds up his free hand to show me grubby nails and palms stained gray from the daily grime of living rough.

"Grayson, think about this," he pleads, his eyes dropping to his feet. "We're from different worlds. Look at you and your custom cut clothes and your million-dollar mansion. Then look at me. I'm broke as a convict, and I live in my truck."

I stop walking, but keep a tight hold on his hand as I come about to face him.

"We've temporarily occupied different worlds for a while," I reply in defense of my *very good* idea, reminding him just how wrong he is. "We're from the same place, right here in Abingdon and Jackson Academy. We grew up not even five blocks away from each other. We had all the same teachers and, until we left for college, we read all the same books, listened to all the same tunes, and shared damn near every thought."

I step up close against him, laying my one free hand on

his chest. I tip up on my toes to reach him, then press my lips against his as our hips come together, our cocks pressing firm against one another. He's hard as steel, and I can feel that his body aches for mine, too.

"The guest bath is at the end of the hall," I huff against his neck, wanting to kiss it and perhaps even nibble. "We're about the same size. I'll bring you a t-shirt and sweat pants. You can do whatever you need. Take your time."

I'm as good as my word, collecting a stack of clean underwear, a t-shirt, and sweats for Liam to wear after he's done showering. I collect his dirty—no, filthy—clothes and put them in the washing machine on the *boil like it came from a medieval leper colony* setting. I add extra color-fast bleach, fabric softener, and detergent, hoping the stew of strong chemistry will kill whatever infections and infestations linger in Liam's clothes.

If I have anything to do with it, he and Beau have spent their last night without a legit roof overhead. A hot shower and a comfortable, clean bed should be a human right. I'm embarrassed that I live (to the extreme of privilege and comfort) in a country where people don't have access to even the most basic human necessities and comforts, and are taught from the time they're old enough to walk that it's their own fault they are poor, lonely, and hungry. I'm not reminded of it often enough. But looking at Liam... I can tell he *does* come from a different world. And it was a terrible set of circumstances that led him to this life.

Is it Liam's fault he was steamrolled by a guy who outweighed him by ninety pounds? Is it his fault the only thing he was ever really great at was football, and once that was gone, there was nothing to fall back on?

It's not his fault. It was a trap that was set for him in his childhood. It's just like the trap set for me that's stealing every single spare second of my time, making it nearly impossible for me to have a life beyond work. When I take time off, which is almost never, the board of directors and everyone on my executive team behaves as if I'm stealing. None of them can fathom a Silicon Valley CEO who isn't plugged in 24-7.

As soon as I saw Liam tonight, I put my phone on silent. It's going to stay that way until I decide to re-engage.

Liam's shower promises to be of some duration, so I have time for one of my own. Following mine, I'm checking on my supplies stash, including lube and condoms, when Liam appears wearing just a pair of my Calvin boxers and an enigmatic smile. Beau is with him, trailing a few inches behind.

"I told him to stay but he came up anyway," Liam states apologetically. "Is it okay? He's not used to being away from home."

Home being a pick-up truck? Nobody ever looked so damned good in my shorts. He's smoother than a fresh jar of Skippy, and I want to eat him up.

"Beau's good," I assure him, my cock stiffening again just looking at him. "Come get in bed. If you're okay with that."

Liam looks at me hesitantly. "I'm not rich, Gray. Far from it." I can tell he's hard already, through the outline of his clothes. "I want to. But I'm... far from the Liam you used to know."

I lean forward. "Then let me know you again."

I reach out for him, and he steps toward me.

CHAPTER TWO

LIAM

*T*his probably isn't going to end well. It makes no sense at all for me to be here. That said, when have I ever let good sense guide me?

Nobody's touched me like Grayson just touched me, since… *well…* since the last time Grayson touched me almost a decade ago. His fingers are electric. His touch makes my heart skip. My breath catches in my chest and my diaphragm seizes with a jolt.

He pulls back the covers and sheets on his sprawling king-sized bed, beckoning me toward it.

"Climb in," he says. He crawls in ahead of me, sliding his long, strong legs under the heavy comforter, patting the vacant side for me to join him. His body is exquisite, his eyes intense and wanting and full of need.

Who the hell could ever say 'no' to that? What sane human would want to?

There's no way this can end well.

This is Grayson. He was a kid the last time I saw him: a skinny, self-conscious, awkward kid with a crush and the most disarming smile you ever saw. His smile made my day five days a week when we were kids. I could have had a shitty weekend with foster parents and a house full of kids just as lost as I was, and then I'd see Grayson smiling at me from across the parking lot. I would melt, every time I saw him. It's impossible to be mad or blue when you see that smile beaming at you.

I knew he was crushing on me back then, but I was almost three years older than him, and it would have been wrong to go there. He was too young and too... *earnest.* Too sweet.

He's not too young anymore, and it's clear he knows exactly what he's about.

I crawl onto the bed on my hands and knees, stalking straight up to him.

"You're sure about this?" I ask, checking in for the last time before I give up and give in.

Grayson grins, reaching forward, cupping his hand around my head, pulling me to him.

"I'm damn sure," he replies. "I'm only sorry it took us so long to get here."

I have no idea what I'm doing. I haven't gotten laid in so long it doesn't even seem like a memory – more like a dream I imagined. The last guy who made a pass at me was damn near sixty years old, offering a twenty-dollar bill in exchange for a ride in the front seat of his Oldsmobile.

I may be homeless, but I'm not stupid. I decided I'd rather go hungry.

I don't know what Grayson is up to. I don't know who he is now, since he's been on the cover of *Fortune* and is referenced weekly on *Bloomberg.* All I know is we have deep history, and he's all grown up. He remembers me and he wants this, *so...* I've got nothing to lose except pristine memories of our adolescent friendship. And that, frankly, isn't seeming so important right now.

"Come here," Grayson says, pulling me on top of him as he lies back in the crisp, fragrant sheets.

I have no bank account... I've got thirty dollars to my name and I need to buy dog food... I need new tires on the truck because the ones on there now are bald... And I'm in bed, getting naked with my best friend from high school who just so happens to be a billionaire Silicon Valley CEO with his own company and a gazillion dollars in contracts from the military and automotive corporations.

It doesn't matter who Grayson is now. He's still that crazy-smart kid from third period Algebra 2 who offered to help me with my homework if I could show him how to use the weight machines in the gym. I took that deal as a freshman and never regretted the trade. Looking back on it now, it's entirely possible Grayson got the better end of that trade. He's built like a fitness model. He looks good, like a billion dollars, and I'm the one with grime embedded so deep under my nails it'll never come out.

His lips taste like Red Hot candies, almost burning me. His flesh is warm against mine, searing, taut, and ready for my fingers as I glide them over it, searching.

"Tell me what we're doing," I whisper, dropping to Grayson's ear. "Tell me what you want."

"All of it," he huffs, his breath scorching against my shoulder. "All of it, and then more of it."

"I can do that," I say. I moan softly into him. He smells of the sky and the mountains, of white pine and rosemary. He smells like home.

Grayson is no longer the skinny, insecure kid I knew in high school. I always knew he'd grow up and out of that awkward stage, but only in my most private moments did I allow myself to imagine he and I might grow into a moment like this.

Even when I was in college and experimenting, on the

down-low, I was fumbling and unsure, always worried about getting caught and getting outed. I never learned the fear-lessness that Grayson has now. I never progressed to the unchecked assertiveness he's showing me now.

He presses his hand against my chest, pushing me back-ward. Then in a quick, one-two move I don't see coming, he flips me over on my back and he's on top, grinning down on me like he just scored points. His body is long, lithe, and beautiful. It's sexy as fuck looking up at him, knowing what he wants to do to me. My cock is doing all my thinking for me. I'm hard, damn near ripping through these nice Jockey shorts I found in Grayson's closet.

He reaches down, his fingers slipping under the waist-band, then circling around my length. The sensation is enough to make me swoon – or nearly cum right in his grip. I close my eyes, searing them shut, my breath catching in my chest. I need to concentrate hard or this isn't going to last. It's been too damn long since anyone's been this close.

He strokes me, taking his time, teasing my full length out. Then he slips his fingers behind my sack, gently rolling my balls in his hand.

"I'm going to go down on you," he whispers, leaning into my neck, his words hot and wet against my skin. "And it's okay if you blow fast because we won't be done. I want your ass. Is that okay?"

Just listening to the words very nearly makes me drop my load. I can't respond. I just nod, my eyes closed, my breath held. "Yes, yes... that's okay... Oh *my* God..."

His mouth is on me, hot and tight, his tongue expertly working up from the base of my shaft to my tip. I think I forgot what this felt like. Maybe I needed to, or I would have gone crazy missing it. He sucks me deep, lapping my length into his throat, swallowing the head of my cock again and again while his curious fingertips explore my ass. My balls grow tight, drawn up and about to explode.

"Oh, for fuck's sake," I groan, feeling the pressure back up, the heat rise behind my cock, tensing my asshole, making my knees weak, and my hands tremble.

I cum a few seconds later with a magnificent explosion deep in Grayson's throat and loud exclamations. Beau hears me and howls in response. I just hang onto Grayson's head and shoulders, gripping, grabbing at anything I can get a hold of until the frantic moment has passed; until he has pulled away, hanging above me looking down into my liquid eyes, his eyes smiling – almost laughing – at me.

I feel tears running down the sides of my face. Nothing has ever felt that perfect before. No one has ever looked at me like Grayson is looking at me right now.

"Oh, you haven't seen anything yet," he croons, lifting fingers to touch my face softly. "I'm going to treat you so good, you're never going to want to let me go."

I'm already there.

A few minutes later and Grayson has me backed up to his hips, my ass spread wide to his invading, pumping cock. He wasn't altogether gentle about it, but after a fleeting moment of shock I surrendered to the torturous, maddening, all-consuming pleasure of being properly fucked by a man who authentically knows what he's doing back there.

I'm immobilized in his grip; his strong arms and hands hold my shoulders down, drawing my whole body back against his in time with his driving pelvic thrusts. When he draws back, his length scrubs against that little nut just inside my cavity, sending ricocheting wave after wave of pleasure rippling from my toe tips to the top of my head and back.

Much more of this and I'll come again. My length – fully recovered already and standing up firm – demands attention.

Grayson doesn't miss his chance to fuck me hard in the ass, while reaching around to stroke me.

"God damn," he hisses, his teeth grazing my neck, his fist pounding my hip. "God damn…"

His super-heated shaft swells inside me then erupts, pouring a tidal wave of his essence into me, the excess spilling out the lip of the condom. His hot breath, heavy and wet, stings my salty skin as his body slides over mine, driving deep inside me again and again until he's limp and spent.

But I'll be damned if that's all there is.

Grayson rolls off me, eyes bleary, expression slightly dazed. He reaches down and slips off the condom, absently tying it off and tossing it toward the trash can – *and missing.* I kiss him hard, nicking his lips, then reach over him to the box of condoms, grabbing the bottle of lube.

"On your knees," I instruct him, rolling him face down, then drawing his ass back towards me before Grayson really knows what's going on. "My turn."

His hands come up, pushing down onto the mattress as if he's doing a plank. I reach forward, shoving him back down, hiking his hips up, pulling his strong legs backward.

"Relax," I urge him, one hand stroking his back, the other holding his hip in my solid grip.

"Easy," he huffs, his tone tight with anxiety. "I'm not used to bottoming."

Shocking. The billionaire likes to top.

"Neither was I," I say. "But it was pretty fucking awesome. So just relax."

He fights it and fights me until he's turned over and we're face to face. Once there, he relents, relaxing, drawing his knees up to his chest, giving me unfettered access.

Using my fingers and a gracious plenty of lube, I gradu-ally work his opening wider and wider until it's almost relaxed enough to admit me. I slather a glob of slick goodness all over my dick, from head to balls, then I press in. Slipping past Grayson's tight rim, into the dark, hot cave of his perfection, it's a secret bliss. I lose all sense of time and place. Instead, shoving into his hard body deeper and deeper, feeling myself disappear into him more and more completely.

It's been so long since I was anywhere close to this place. I cannot recollect what it means or who I even am. The pleasure is supernatural. The distraction is complete. I could fuck like this until the end of time... except it feels too damn good.

"Oh fuck," Grayson cries, reaching around for my hand. He grabs it and, before I even know what's happened, my hand is wrapped around his cock. With his hand wrapped around mine, he's stroking himself, using my hand to do it. He tightens my grip on him, extending the length of my stroke, which makes me draw back further then shove in deeper from behind.

"Of fuck!" he cries again, his body tensing.

He's going to cum. The knowledge of which is enough to make me cum. I can't stop it or control it. I unload hard and complete, shoving in deep until there's almost nothing left to give. That's when Grayson hits release, returning the gesture. He spills his load on my hand, on the sheets, and on the pillows, spreading a sticky, hot mess everywhere from my hands and his belly, to the wallpaper behind the bed.

"Oh, fuck!" Grayson shudders, his body convulsing against mine, eyes seared closed, a shattered cry escaping his lips. His fingers, which were locked tight around my upper arms digging in so deep I'm sure they left marks, relax, releasing, slipping away. His entire body goes limp, deflating. His expression softens to an easy, thoughtless smile.

"Damn," he huffs dreamily, eyes opening, pupils blown and unfocused.

He trembles again, flexing, as I gently pull out. After slipping off the condom, tying it off, and dropping it in the wastebasket beside the bed, I roll off to Grayson's side, propping up on an elbow, peering down at him. High quality orgasms are like magical time machines; they take years off your age. Grayson – breathing shallow and regular beside me – looks about seventeen years-old now instead of twenty-eight and change. He looks like that boy I knew back when, except now he's got the perfect physique of a very fit young man.

He's so beautiful it almost hurts to look at him. It would be so easy to fall into those arms again and again, but I need to be realistic about what this is – *and what it isn't.*

"Ummm," he mumbles, turning into my chest. His left leg hikes up over my hip, hooking his heel behind my knee. He pulls me close to him as he relaxes, snuggling into me. "Sleep. Sleep."

What is this? Grayson is going to sleep curled up against my chest. He's purring like a kitten. *What in the world do I do with that?*

Behind me I hear a familiar whine and the sound of Beau's nails padding on the hardwood floor. A moment later his cold nose pokes into my back. He stands up, putting his front paws on the edge of the bed. I roll back toward him while trying my best not to disturb Grayson.

"Lay down," I tell Beau, but he's not interested in my commands. He smells clean sheets and sees the warm covers. He wants in.

Before I can stop him he leaps up, jumping onto the bed.

"Beau! No!" I cry quietly. "Get down."

Grayson stirs, smiling in his sleep, wrapping his arms around my chest.

"He's okay," he whispers. "Let him stay. I like dogs."

Beau sniffs, then circles around a couple times before

settling down into a tight, comfortable curl behind my knees. He's used to making do with a crusty patch of sleeping bag jammed into the corner of the bed of my pickup, so this is puppy-love paradise. I reach behind me, touching the crown of his head with extended fingers, massaging him between the ears. Beau lifts his noggin, nuzzles my hand, licking me in gratitude for the luxurious digs.

"Not my doing, buddy," I assure him. "But yeah, way better than the truck. Warmer too."

I lay my head down a few moments later, my eyes fixed on Grayson's peaceful countenance. I'm not sure when I finally let go and find sleep, but sleep comes quicker and more deeply than I expected. When I next open my eyes, the sun shines in through open blinds filtered through the flittering shadow of leaves from the trees outside beyond the window.

I bolt up in bed, shocked. At first, I don't know where I am. Then it all comes flooding back in: drinks and pizza. And then. Other things too.

Beau lifts his big ol' head. Sad, cautious eyes peer up at me as if he's not sure whether to keep pretending to sleep or get up and find a corner to pee in. He's bound to need to go.

We are alone.

I roll out of bed, looking for my clothes. I find them in the bathroom, folded and stacked neatly, freshly washed and dried, smelling like fancy laundry detergent. After a very quick shower, I dress. I'm silently freaking out, worried about the inevitable awkward moment that's going to transpire the second Grayson reappears.

I'll make it easy on both of us. I'll bolt as soon as I can get my shoes on.

I'm coming down the stairs with Beau on my heel when Grayson appears below, looking up at us.

"I thought I heard you," he says, smiling. He's dressed in

dark, expensive jeans and an Oxford cloth button down, untucked, with bare feet. He looks good, even dressed like a preppy douche. "Let's go get some breakfast. I'm starving."

He's either being really polite, or he's delusional. The only place open for Sunday Brunch is the Tavern, and it's where Abingdon's A-listers congregate on Sunday mornings. If we went there, he would be the topic du jour among the ladies who gossip--and not in a good way.

"Sorry," I say, keeping my tone congenial and upbeat. "I can't. Gotta get Beau home and fed. Gotta get some work done."

Grayson's brow furrows. He sets his jaw *just so*, as if he doesn't know what to make of my statement.

"What?"

I breeze past him, heading for the door, feeling the color rising to my face as recollections of all the things we did together creep into my consciousness. I recall his cock and how unbelievably great it felt buried deep inside me. That's not all I recall.

"Come on," Grayson says, meeting me, then turning with me as I pass because I don't pause. I'm on a mission. "Just brunch. I'll drive you back to…"

He's being way more polite than he needs to be.

I shake him off. "Sorry."

"At least give me your number," he protests, following me onto the front porch. "How do I get in touch with you?"

I hustle down the steps trying hard not to let him know I'm interested.

"I don't have a phone," I admit. "I'm around. Everyone worth knowing knows how to get up with me. Just ask around."

"At least let me drive you wherever you're going," Grayson calls out behind me. "Why are you in such a hurry?"

I raise my arm, not turning back. "Places to be," I call back. "We're used to walking. Thanks though."

Beau's with me, keeping close as I get away, leaving Grayson to watch us walk off across the lawn toward the driveway and the main road. I manage to escape without either of us having to revisit those awkward moments or make idle small talk. We both got what we wanted: a fun night to put some old fantasies to the test and to final rest. Now I can put Grayson Ellis out of my mind once and for all.

* * *

IT'S A LONG, not fun hike down country roads in the building heat, but Beau and I are no strangers to inconvenience. He pads alongside me, keeping pace, his tongue hanging out like he's about to die of thirst, giving me backward glances like his feelings are hurt.

"I'm thirsty too," I tell him, wiping sweat off my brow with the back of my hand. I was all sweet-smelling and clean when we left Grayson this morning, but after this hike in the heat, I'm going to be a stinky, grimy mess all over again.

I left the truck parked in the lot behind one of the restaurants downtown. That's all well and good until downtown wakes up and somebody notices my beat-to-shit truck left where it isn't supposed to be and I'm not asleep inside of it to explain it being there. I've been towed before like that, and that sucks. At the moment, I wouldn't have the cash to get it back, and Beau's dog food is in the truck. He'd never forgive me if there wasn't a big bowl of chow at the end of this long, winding road.

After hoofing it for an hour, we make it back to town. All my paranoia is answered with a flood of relief when we turn the block at that popular Cajun restaurant and I see my truck rusting in place right where I left it. Beau perks up, his tail lifting with the spiky hairs on his back. He starts wagging and trotting faster toward home.

He gets food and water before I do anything else. He laps up a bowlful of fresh water in no time flat, asking for more even though half of what I gave him is spilled all over the pavement.

"You're such a mess," I scold him. "Wasteful. Bottled water's not cheap. Go easy."

Today is laundry day, so while Beau has his breakfast I climb into the bed of the truck, under the camper top, scrounging for dirty clothes. They're everywhere.

I stuff random shirts and socks into my frayed pillow case, searching under grocery bags and behind a case of water for my favorite shirt: an old Virginia Tech practice jersey with my last name and number on it.

I find it balled up and shoved in the back corner under a towel. It's threadbare and stained, faded badly, but it's all I've got left of the brightest days of my life when playing college ball seemed like it was just one step up on an ever-ascending ladder. When I wore that jersey, running plays and running circles around everyone else on the field, I was sure I was going places. I lived the life of a prince when I was at Tech. Everyone knew me. Everyone wanted to hang out with me. I got invited to all the best parties. All the prettiest girls wanted to date me – and the prettiest boys too.

My picture was on calendars and coffee mugs. I auto-graphed ticket stubs and game day programs for fans and alumni, and I even got interviewed on ESPN a half-dozen times. I was the golden boy who was a first round draft pick, then traded twice, landing with the second-best team in the NFL before the week was out.

I told my coach at Tech and the coach of the Patriots I was going to finish my senior year.

If I'd known then what I know now, I would have walked

away from school the day the Patriots punched my card. I was trying to do the right thing. In the end, none of them did the right thing by me. I was good at one thing: playing football. Once I couldn't play, they were all done with me.

I remember being just a day or two out of surgery, loaded up on painkillers, and being put on a medical transport to Abingdon's Johnston Memorial Hospital to recuperate. Nobody at Tech was concerned with my rehabilitation or whether I walked again. It took an orthopedic nurse who had been a fan of mine to call in specialists from Bristol to get me even a fraction of the support I needed to get back on my feet.

The Virginia Tech boosters put together a GoFundMe to pay my physical therapy bill. They raised twenty-eight hundred dollars. The bill was close to twenty-thousand. I still owe all that money. There's no way in hell I'll ever be able to pay it back.

I grab my grimy Tech jersey, shoving it in the pillow case with the rest of my dirty clothes, then call Beau to jump in the cab as I gather his food and water bowls. I think back on those bleak days after 'the hit' when my leg folded underneath me the wrong way.

Grayson tried to visit me in the hospital. I told them to send him away.

I was in pain, sick on painkillers, and sick in my heart. I had steel pins in my leg and seeping wounds where the shattered bones sliced through my skin. I was depressed and scared, and I was totally alone.

I don't know why I made them send him away. Maybe I was just trying to disappear.

Well, he found me. It took a while, but he finally found me.

The heat rises to my cheeks when I think of what we did last night. That's the last thing I expected when I headed out to collect beer bottles and cans from the streets and side-walks. I would have laid low if I'd known Grayson was in town.

I must have been out of my mind. He's got to be thanking his lucky stars I left. He was probably terrified I was going to try and linger like some kind of gold-digging stalker. Guys like Grayson like their fun, but they also know when to cut bait. There's no way in hell Grayson Ellis meant to hang out with me. Guys like him know better than to get tangled up with losers like me.

Beau sits up in his seat, looking at me, cocking his head. He's smiling.

"What?" I ask.

He lifts his muzzle and barks, then drops down, resting his massive head in my lap with one paw up. He loves me. *He adores me.* No matter how big of a fuck-up I am, h*e forgives me*.

"Love you too, buddy," I assure him, resting my hand on his head. I gently rub his crown, fondling his floppy ears. "Love you so much."

Beau licks my hand, pressing his paw against my belly.

Beau's my best friend in the world. He's all I have that really matters, and the only reason I even bother waking up in the morning.

CHAPTER THREE

GRAYSON

his morning I got a call from Naomi, my PA, giving me a heads-up that Tony is on his way here, courtesy of the Board of Directors, to 'find out what's going on.'

I knew it wouldn't take long for the red flags to start coming up, but I really hoped to avoid Tony getting involved. He can be... *challenging*... especially when he feels empowered by the board to get involved.

Tony and I were best friends in college. On paper, he's a co-founder of the company. He's got the title of Chief Operating Officer, which basically means he floats all over the place. The board uses him as a hatchet man and a fixer. He's good at both roles when we need those services. But when we don't, Tony can get in the way. He's a hammer. Most days we need a laser scalpel.

In his defense, Tony was essential to me when I first envisioned the company. He was my lead cheerleader, salesman, and door opener. I was a geeky kid with a southern accent and crazy ideas about sustainable energy and batteries. Tony took my ideas and made them sound sensible to everyday people. He made them look like a great investment. He – with nothing more than his charm, good looks, and uber-confidence – convinced the world we were legitimate.

That was ten years ago. The company and its client list have grown exponentially. Tony's skillset hasn't.

The company, Theos Universal, is publicly traded on the New York Stock Exchange. Just like the Ford Motor Company, Walmart, and dozens of other multi-billion dollar corporations, it's still largely held in private hands. I own forty-eight percent of all the stock in the company. The next closest owner is an institutional investment fund holding eight percent. When they started buying up blocks of shares in Theos, I started buying up blocks of their shares. I now control fifty-two percent of the company that owns eight percent of mine. My strategic holdings make it all but impossible for anything to happen at Theos without my knowledge and consent, but that doesn't mean it's run like a dictatorship. *I wish.*

I have to fight for everything I want to accomplish, and I'm constantly fighting to keep the company from being driven into the rocks by executives who can't see beyond the next quarterly report. The Board of Directors often falls into the rut of short-term thinking. All they care about is the bottom line, *right now.* They're rarely interested in working today for tomorrow's greater reward.

"You asked me to lunch to tell me what you have going on," Mel says, stabbing her bed of leafy greens with a fork. "Now you're just staring at your phone like the Oracle of Delphi is in it, about to impart some killer wisdom. What gives?"

I put my phone face down on the table. She's right. Mel is always right.

"I'm working on a covert deal to sell the company," I blurt out, happy to unleash the secret. "More like a merger," I clarify. "Whatever it's called, I'm trying to get the details worked out before the story leaks. The board doesn't know about it. I don't want our customers to get wind of it. I need to keep this under wraps until the details are done."

Mel stops chewing. She gazes at me a long time, her expression blank, eyes unblinking.

"Why are you doing this?" she finally asks. "And who would I tell?"

I shrug. "Nobody, I say. "I'm doing it because I'm tired."

There's a bigger excuse though, and I need to own it. "And the federal contracts are getting too big. I didn't build this company so we could supply the Pentagon with better power supplies for their weapon systems. If we get absorbed by a larger company, all the contracts will have to be renegotiated. It'll slow things down a bit."

"You're such an idealist," Mel observes, chewing greens, sending them down slow as she considers what I've said. "Won't the company buying your company just make new contracts?"

I nod my head. "Probably," I admit. "But at least it won't be my name on the contract anymore."

"That's admirable," Dexter, Mel's fiancé, contributes between bites of Reuben sandwich. It's the first time he's spoken since we arrived. "If everyone thought like you, we'd live in a better world."

Probably not.

"Hey, isn't that the pretty vagrant you hooked up with at Buskerfest?" Mel observes, craning her neck up to catch a better look. She nods toward the front and a guy – Liam – carrying boxes to his truck parked just beyond the restaurant's main entrance.

While I'm watching Liam, trying to decide how to respond to my sister, the front door opens and Tony Carraro steps inside, looking around.

Shit. He spots me instantly, lifting his hand, nodding, coming this way.

Just then my phone rings. The caller ID says it's Justin Trivet, the CEO of Nicolai Automotive — the company I'm clandestinely negotiating the sale with. *How the hell can all of this be happening at one time?*

I lift my phone, swiping to answer.

"Hey, it's me," I say, motioning to Mel that I have to take the call, while getting up and moving toward the door. "Give me thirty seconds to get clear of the restaurant noise."

I meet Tony with an expression communicating all my displeasure at seeing him in Abingdon.

"I'm having lunch with my sister and her fiancé," I say, backing him into the waitstaff cubby where we can't be seen, holding my phone close to my chest so Justin can't hear us. "This is personal time, not company time. You're welcome to join us, but no business talk. At all. Understood?"

Tony nods, surprised at the lack of cordial greeting. "Yeah," he says. "You okay?"

"I'm great," I tell him. "Now I've got to take this call. Excuse me."

"Who is it?" he asks, pressing his luck like he always does.

I glare at him, walking away, gliding through the kitchen and out the door. I swing around the corner, down an ally to where the restaurant's dumpsters are parked. It smells like bad fish and rotting vegetables.

Justin has called to assure me he received all the financial data I sent and that Nicolai's accountants are reviewing it.

"Give us some time," he says. "I've had to keep this quiet internally and part of that means it's a small group working on the review and analysis. It takes longer."

"It's all good," I tell him. "Let's just complete the initial due diligence as fast as we can. I'm trying to bypass the trouble makers, but it's just a matter of time until they're onto me. They're already sending out feelers to find out what I have going on."

"That was inevitable," Justin laughs. "Using your sister's engagement party for cover was brilliant, but it only lasts so long. You need a funeral to attend, or something."

Or something. I give Justin my regards as I end the call. When I get back to my table, Tony's got Mel and Dexter in stitches, telling them some story about me. It's a riot, I'm sure.

I look up and see Liam load a box into the back of his truck, then slam the tailgate shut like he's finished and about to go.

"Excuse me," I say to Mel. "I need to go talk to someone about something."

Liam hasn't called me or texted. Contrary to what he said, no one I know knows how to get in touch with him. I got some strange looks when asking about him. But here he is in the flesh (sweet flesh that it is) and I'll be damned if I'm going to let him slip away again.

I'm not accustomed to chasing a ghost like Liam Gold. I'm much more accustomed to trying to ditch my own stalkers. I don't exactly know what to say or how to do this, but I'm determined not to take 'no' for an answer.

"Liam!"

He swings around, dropping his keys on the pavement. He looks at me, then down at his keys, then back up at me. Finally, he bends over, retrieving his keys, jamming them in the frayed front pocket of his well-worn jeans.

"Hey Grayson," he says, his eyes averted. His tone is stretched tight with anxiety.

"What the fuck?" I ask him in absolute seriousness. "You ghosted me. You ran away and I haven't heard a peep out of you. It's been over a week."

He blinks, looking to the side. "I didn't...think you *wanted* to see me..." he stutters. "I didn't want to..."

Just then a familiar face appears from inside the cab of Liam's truck. Beau shoves out, standing in the open window, pressing his big head under Liam's arm. He makes eye contact with me, then he huffs and jumps down, straight through the open window, coming to me, rubbing his head in my hand while wagging vigorously.

At least his dog is happy to see me.

"Beau!" Liam chides him. "You'll break a leg jumping out like that!

He grabs the dog by his collar and holds.

"Somebody likes me," I say, dropping to my knees to accept sloppy kisses from Beau. "Yea! Good boy, Beau. Good boy!"

He's wagging so hard his whole butt rocks back and forth. If he goes any harder, he's going to fall over.

I peer up at Liam, marveling at his crystalline gray eyes and the tangle of tattoos wrapping his limbs in color and intricate line.

"Why didn't you call me?" I ask him, my expression and tone imploring. "Was I that bad? That you had to run away?"

CHAPTER FOUR

LIAM

*G*ood God! *Is that what he thinks?* That sad expression on his face looks more hurt than angry.

I pull Beau back to the truck, opening the door, telling him to get in. Once he's in, I roll the window halfway up so he can't escape again. He rests his head on the edge of the glass, his big brown eyes staring me, pouting. I scratch his withers and then turn back to Grayson.

I could make up a hundred excuses. None of them would be plausible and he'd know I was lying. Or, I could just suck up my pride – what broken shards are left of it – and tell him the truth.

"If I had, what would eventually come of it?" I ask him, posing a reasonable question. Beau whines behind me. "We could hook up a few more times – and it was great, by the way – but soon you're going back to your very big life, leaving me to mine. We don't exactly run in the same social circles, y'know?"

Grayson rises from his crouch on the sidewalk where he was petting Beau. He crosses his arms over his broad chest, looking a little defensive.

"You don't really know me well enough to know this, so trust me when I tell you I don't run in *any* social circles," Grayson says. "Meeting you again reminded me that should change."

How so?

Grayson takes a step closer, his expression softening.

"Do you really sleep in your truck?" he asks.

I nod, my eyes falling briefly to the pavement at my feet. This situation isn't exactly my fault. I've just never been able to catch a break. I thought that was all going to change when I got the scholarship to Tech. I had four great years, then it was done. The second I tried to get back on my feet, making a living with my hands, somebody broke into my truck and stole my tools.

A carpenter with no tools is a joke.

"I sleep in my truck," I admit. At least I have the truck. Plenty people sleep rough out in the open.

"You said you were working as a carpenter, but your tools got stolen? How do you get by?"

He paid attention. I nod. "Any way possible." I motion to the boxes piled under my camper lid. "I'm cleaning out a building next to the restaurant. I haul everything to the dump. Anything valuable I come across belongs to me. Occasionally I score on something."

Grayson's eyes narrow. His smile flattens. I can see his wheels turning, and I'm not sure I like it.

"You wanna go out with me again?" he asks. "Do you like me?"

What is he about?

"Grayson, you know I do," I say, feeling the futility of all of this. "But I'm a broke, homeless guy with zero prospects. I don't shower regularly. We're not…"

"That's not what I asked," he says, interrupting. "I asked if you *wanted* to. What if all these problems you see as insur-

44

mountable and definitive of who you are, are just things I see as temporary embarrassments to a guy I've known as one of the kindest, brightest, hardest working, dearest friends I've ever had?"

What's he saying? "Ummm."

"Liam, what are you doing in two hours?"

"I need to haul this stuff to the dump. After that, I'm free," I tell him.

"Meet me right here in two hours," Grayson states, not asking. "Don't be late."

He hugs me – surprising me – then excuses himself back into the restaurant just as quickly as he appeared.

Grayson Ellis is up to something. I don't exactly know what it is, but I suspect it involves me behaving like an average human, bathing daily, and sleeping under a roof that isn't attached to a combustion-engine powered vehicle.

I back up to my truck, leaning on the door, reaching up to press my open fingers against Beau's muzzle.

"He's cooking up something," I say, turning to look at my best buddy. "You up for that? It might mean big changes."

Beau raises his head, wagging his tail. He likes Grayson. Beau's always been an excellent judge of character. I guess I should trust Beau and not doubt Grayson, but it's hard to trust. It's especially hard when Grayson is being such a high-handed control freak.

"Don't be late," I repeat to Beau, mocking Grayson's presumptive tone. "Like he's something so special to be all punctual for."

He is though, as much as I don't want to admit it.

CHAPTER FIVE

GRAYSON

*S*ome days it sucks being me, and some days it's great being me. Right now, I'm not sure which it is. It'll depend on how the rest of this afternoon goes.

If I can get Theos successfully merged with Nicolai Motor Corp, getting myself unwound from the daily operations of the company I conceived and founded, I'll have a lot more time to reacquaint myself with my hometown, my sister, her fiancé, our parents, and a life beyond ninety-hour work weeks and flying all over the world to make sure things run smoothly. I'm sick of making the "Twenty Under Thirty CEOs to Watch" list, having no life of my own, constantly stressed out by directors, shareholders, and stock valuations. My twenties have been consumed with ambition and anxiety. I'm determined my thirties are going to be different.

A few weeks spent in Abingdon has served to remind me just how different – and better – my world might be if I could just get free of Silicon Valley success. Elias Spaulding did it, shedding his corporate shackles and finding love, life, and a place to settle down. He's with his kid, his husband. He's fucking happy.

I want that too.

Turning my rental car onto Main Street, I spy Liam's rusted old Toyota parked at the end of the block, him leaning against the driver's side door, arms folded across his broad chest, his long legs dressed in frayed, faded denim. My mind can't help but wander. I wonder what he'd look like in a tailored silk suit. His feet are wrapped in dirty work boots, but I bet he'd sport a pair of handmade Ferragamos with the best of them. Guys who look like Liam shouldn't have to shop at thrift stores. If I have my way, the stylists will come to him begging for an opportunity to dress him.

I pull the Audi alongside him and roll down the window.

"Get in," I say. "Got some things to show you."

Liam seems doubtful. He uncrosses his arms, leaning down into my open window. "Where are we going?" he asks. "How long will we be?"

I peer past him, seeing Beau in the cab of the truck.

"Bring Beau," I say. "He can get in the back."

"You didn't answer my question," Liam observes, unmoved. "Where are we going?"

Only in Abingdon, beggars are choosers and the homeless need particulars regarding their delivery from oblivion.

"My place," I tell him. "All twelve thousand square feet of it, and all the renovation work the place needs. I need your opinion on priorities."

His expression betrays him. He's intrigued.

"I can't leave Beau here," he says. "We'll come out sometime later."

"Beau can come now," I repeat. "Get in."

I watch Liam struggle to come up with more excuses. He hedges, jaw set, eyes rolling like he knows he's caught.

"Get in," I insist. "Beau too."

It's only a ten-minute drive out across the lake to my

place, but Liam makes the most of those few minutes by piling on with the protests.

"I don't even know what this is about," he says. "My advice on what this place needs is ten years old and about as useful as any high school kid's opinion. You can hire someone who knows what they're doing. You're playing me, and it's not cool."

I smirk, cutting my eyes at him briefly. "I don't recall you bellyaching so much back in high school," I say. "I'm not playing you, and you know it. You know me, Liam. Have I ever played you – or anybody?"

He scowls, turning his attention to the early autumn scenery flying by at fifty miles per hour.

"I haven't seen you in ten years," he says. "I hardly know you anymore. All I know is you're loaded, and I don't have a good track record with people who have money. When push comes to shove, they've never treated me very well."

Finally, something Liam and I can agree on.

"Yeah," I say. "But I'm not them. And if you'll give me a chance, I'm going to prove that to you."

Liam huffs a cynical laugh. "Oh yeah?" he asks. "How are you gonna do that?"

I have nothing to lose by offering, so I do.

"I'm going to offer you the job of overseeing the renovation of the lake house," I tell him. "You used to be a pretty great carpenter, and I know you know how to run a job. You did it when we were kids, working for your uncle. This time it's just one house instead of an entire subdivision."

Liam turns away from the window, wide eyes staring at me. He doesn't say anything for the longest time. When he finally does speak, I'm disappointed by his response.

"I can't," he says, his tone insistent. "I told you, I don't have any tools. I've got no way to move supplies. I don't even own a laptop for tracking estimates and expenses. I'm not

48

qualified. If you need a contractor, I know plenty. I'll give you a referral."

I decide not to respond immediately. Instead, I determine to let the house work its magic for me.

"This is ridiculous, Grayson," Liam complains. "You should just take me back to my truck."

I pull off the highway onto the narrow, paved drive winding up to the house. In daylight, the house – perched high on a prospect overlooking the lake – looks majestic. It's like something from a movie set, with scores of windows surveying the property. Recessed porches and porticos, peppered high and low, sit around each wing of the house.

"Her bones are solid," I tell Liam. "The previous owner did some work to it in the early 1970s that would have been better had it been left undone, but it is what it is. Other than that, nothing's been done since the late 1920s when the kitchen and baths were added and it was wired for electric."

Liam's brow peaks. "The wiring is original?" he asks.

I nod, pleased he's concerned.

"Yeah," I say, pulling into the parking area behind the house. "Is that a problem?"

As we depart the car and make our way inside, Liam launches into a ten minute long sermon on the need to get the electric up to code and the risk of a fire it poses in its current condition. As soon as he takes a breath, I interject, "Okay, the wiring is a priority. That goes to the top of the list. Now, let me show you the rest of the house."

He spent the night a few weeks back, but he didn't hang around long enough to get the grand tour. This time I'm making sure he sees everything up close and personal. Once upon a time, Liam spent hours fantasizing about getting a close look at this old place and then getting his hands dirty fixing it up. Now is his chance. He's just got to allow himself the opportunity.

Instead of taking him in via the mud room and kitchen, the way we came in when he was here last, I lead Liam toward the formal garden on the east side. The view of the orchard from that location is stunning, especially this time of year when the trees are wrapped up with green apples. In another month they'll be ripe and sweet, ready for eating and making cider.

The garden is contained inside a shoulder-high wall built of locally quarried granite stones stacked and set in place without mortar. Green moss grows dense in the seams between the blocks, giving the impression of an ancient English garden. It's not the only feature of this place that's reminiscent of an old English country house. The architectural style of the house is distinctly old-world. And given the fact that the house has had no major updates in eighty years or more, there's a shabbiness to it that speaks to the arrogant unwillingness to change so common among the aristocracy.

The garden is overgrown and weedy, but the realtor assured me that beneath the tangle of Virginia Creeper and poison ivy, there are tea roses, daffodils, tulips, begonias, and a host of other colorful flowering species. This winter, when everything has died back, I plan to bring in a professional gardening crew to clear out the overgrowth and prepare a garden using what's already there as well as new things that work with the existing plantings.

"I know a great landscape designer who can help you out with this space," Liam says, completely unsolicited as we traipse through the tangle, stepping over vines. "I bet there's a fortune in flowering bulbs and exotic ornamentals underneath all the weeds. You should bring all that out."

"You think so?" I ask him. "Just looks like a pile of overgrowth to me."

Liam slows, pausing by a tumble of broken branches and flowing tendrils. "Look under there," he says, pointing to a tight clump of fuzzy green leaves clinging low to the ground. "That's phlox, a big spread of it. In the spring and early summer, it blooms a beautiful pink to lavender depending upon the variety and the soil quality. It's a beautiful ground cover."

He takes a few moments to show me row after row of what he believes are irises and more rows of tulips. "I think these are hyacinth," he says, motioning toward clusters of sharp, green leaves poking through the soil. "You're going to have a beautiful garden here once you get all the crowding weeds and vines removed."

I'm astonished at just how much Liam knows about what's in my garden, and pleased he's taking an interest in this project. He seems to have forgotten his protests. Once we get inside the house, it's the same story.

The garden walkway leads to a portico on the east side, offering a lovely view of the valley on one side and the lake on the other. One day this space is going to make a great party area. It's perfect for entertaining on a hot summer night when the cool air rolls in off the lake, catching in a low breeze under the vaulted ceiling of the portico. The tile floors and walls are lovely, shimmering in the light, with sound echoing sharply off their bright surfaces. The space is perfect for eating, drinking, dancing, or just hanging out.

"Wow," Liam exclaims, slowing his pace, peering up at the intricate tile work above our heads. "This is so beautiful."

Beau pauses with Liam, sitting down on his haunches right beside his master, looking up expectantly, waiting for Liam to move again.

"It is," I agree. "But it's in fine shape. I want to show you the work that needs to be done."

I start in the basement with the century-old boiler that functions (or rather doesn't) for a heating system. It's a rusted, leaky, bucket of bolts. So far, I've been able to keep warm using the fireplaces and space heaters, but a few more weeks and this house is going to be uninhabitable due to the cold.

"It's on its last leg," I tell Liam, who stares at the massive antique with wide, unblinking eyes. "I want it ripped out and replaced with a modern, efficient HVAC. At least some of the power source should come from solar and wind. It would be great if we could be completely self-sufficient."

I have much more to show him, so we continue the tour: moving on to the crazy hack of an electrical panel that's probably the biggest fire risk in the county. Liam blanches at the thing, turning white with fright. He takes a breath, then reaches forward, touching a small glass disk screwed in place beside a label reading 'main kitchen'.

He withdraws his hand quickly, cutting his gaze at me. "Do you have somewhere else you can stay tonight?" he asks.

I shake my head. "No," I say. "Why?"

He nods to the electric panel. "That's hot - physically hot to the touch. It's fifty years out of code and wasn't designed to handle the electric pull of modern appliances. You need to just shut it down and get all this ripped out – *now*."

I smile, then nod. "Okay," I say. "But first, let me show you the rest of the project."

There's water damage on the upper floors from a once leaky roof. Plaster walls, molding, ceilings, and hardwood flooring will need to be ripped out and replaced, refinished, and repainted to match all the existing interiors surrounding the damaged spots. There are six bathrooms that need to be brought into the current century, along with repainting the entire interior, making minor repairs, and repairing or replacing the windows and doors.

Once we're back in the kitchen, Liam opens the cabinet doors under one of the sinks and crawls in with his flashlight.

"Damn, skippy!" he calls out. "Copper pipes!"

His head pops out from the under the cabinets. He's grinning from ear to ear. "I'll have to check the whole place just to make sure, but it looks good." He gives me a double thumbs up – which is just devastatingly adorable.

He was expecting lead pipes, which would mean another whole gutting and replacing – a huge, expensive, destructive project. Liam will be pleased to learn that yes, in fact, the house has copper piping throughout.

There are a thousand little things to do here, and ten really big things like the electrical and the HVAC updates. No one person can do them all, but someone who cares about the integrity of the whole house and extended property should oversee the tapestry of work. As far as I'm concerned, Liam's that person. I just need to convince him of the same thing.

"Will you oversee the work?" I ask him straight out. "Act as contractor? Manage the labor, schedule, the budgets, quality control. Everything?"

He looks at me like I'm smoking crack, laughing at me.

"I told you," he says. "I can't. I don't have the tools, or even a fraction of what I'd need to spend my time managing something like this. This is a full-time job for the better part of a year. I have a full-time job just trying to keep warm in my truck."

"What if you had the tools, a nice place to stay, and a vehicle?" I ask. "Even a laptop and smartphone for sending and receiving email and texts from electricians and carpenters? What if I removed all the obstacles?"

He shakes his head, scowling, peering down at the big ridgeback, roan-colored dog who peers up at him with loving, sad eyes.

"I can't," he says again. "Beau's used to being with me all day. I can't leave him…"

"Bring Beau with you," I interrupt, frustrated with his false modesty and recalcitrance. "And look at this."

I walk across the empty room to a window overlooking the northwest side of the property. That side was always hidden from us when we were boys, romanticizing the place from our lounging perch on the far shore.

"What?" Liam asks, stepping up alongside me while keeping a respectful distance. (I wish he'd come closer.)

"There," I point, directing his attention toward a small (by comparison to the rest of the house) bungalow built in a similar style as the main house. It's located a thousand yards west down a dusty, tree lined lane with its back door opening onto a wide grassy field terminating on the edge of a dense copse of trees anchoring the foot of a small mountain. "That's the original overseer's house from when this place was a working plantation," I say. "It was the caretaker's house for decades when this place was vacant."

Liam's brow furrows. He doesn't quite get what I'm proposing.

"Come with me," I say, snapping my fingers to urge Beau along too.

We descend three flights of stairs, taking a shortcut through a hidden passage just off the library. It puts us out on a wide, screened-in porch opening on the narrow lane leading to the small house we saw from the window above. It's only a short hike up the hill to the place.

Up close and personal, the bungalow isn't so small, and it's not stuck in the early part of the last century like the main house.

Liam and Beau follow close on my heels as I mount the steps. Then I slip a key into the front door lock, swinging the door open wide when the bolt turns.

The bungalow has been completely renovated within the last five years, right down to the garden shower in the master bath. The house is mostly furnished with plush couches, chairs, rugs, kitchen things, and even a wide-screen, flat-panel television in a dedicated media room. Liam looks around nervously, then he looks at me.

"What's all this?" he asks, swallowing.

I smile. "Home?" I ask, posing it more as a statement. "Your home. All it needs are sheets and towels and a few personal touches."

He stares at me in disbelief. I choose to let him process the idea in silence. Finally, he breaks his laser lock on my eyes and lets his gaze float around the space, taking it in.

The woodwork in this house isn't quite as elaborate as the main house, but it isn't far off. The rooms are not small, but they're not as obsessively large as those down the lane. The space is intimate, not nearly as drafty as the big house, and it just feels more comfortable.

"Two fifty," I say. "Salary only, first year. You'll have an expense account for materials and travel costs. Oversee the renovation, then stay on as caretaker. What do you say?"

"Two fifty?" Liam asks. "What do you mean?"

He wants more? I should have offered more.

Just then Liam's eyes blow wide open. His whole face animates. He realizes what I've just said.

"Two hundred fifty thousand dollars?" he asks. "To run this job? Are you serious?"

"Yeah," I tell him, nodding, my eyes sharp. "With bonuses for projects delivered on time, under budget. Plus, as a salaried employee, you get three weeks of vacation a year, 401k, and health insurance."

Liam seems stunned, perhaps even ill. He shakes his head as if he cannot fathom what I've offered him: an opportunity to climb out of crushing poverty and homelessness, a chance to reclaim his dignity, earning his own keep in remarkably comfortable circumstances.

"But why?" he asks, the doubt and puzzlement weighing heavy on his tone. "Why me?"

Why him? Why did I buy this house in the first place? Why am I even here? Why did I hire a private detective in an attempt to track him down? Why?

"Liam, isn't that fairly obvious?" I ask him, stepping closer, closing the awkward space between us. I'd take his hand if I wasn't afraid he'd bolt. "Hasn't it been glaringly obvious since we first reconnected?"

He stares at me while his eyes begin – very gradually – to smile, the corners turning up almost imperceptibly. The gray of his irises flash, reflecting a slight lavender tint. He's so beautiful. Just looking at him so closely like this makes my heart almost break.

"Because I'm a really great craft carpenter?" Liam asks, only half-joking. "And you can afford to hire the very best?"

I nod, smiling at his joke. "That's right," I agree. "Only the very best for me."

He nods too, looking around the space once again with wonder in his expression. "A salary, tools, and every-thing..." he mumbles. Then, with a grin, he turns back to me. "If I take this job, are you gonna be one of those bosses who's up my ass all the time about this detail and that, and constantly changing your mind about stuff, making everything and everyone – especially me – crazy?"

I nod, grinning back at him. "I'll be just as far up your ass as you want me," I tease, feeling a bit of bravery rise in my core. I reach for Liam's hand and pull him to me, sliding my other hand around his waist. "And yeah, I'd love to make you just a little bit crazy."

I gently, very respectfully, press my lips to his. I wait for him to soften his stance before parting those sweet, firm lips and allow my tongue to explore. His hot breath sears my lungs, making me dizzy inside his intoxicating taste and scent.

"Are you sure you know what you're doing?" Liam asks me, his voice low, tentative hands coming to rest at my hips. His lips brush my face, breath slipping into my nostrils. "This could get complicated, real fast. You and me, we're worlds apart. People will talk."

I know, and I look forward to it.

"Let 'em talk," I tell him. "I like things complicated. Nothing worthwhile was ever easy."

I reach up. The backs of my fingers push an errant, long lock of blond hair away from his brow. He could use a haircut, but I see no need to point it out; he's probably well aware. And if he's not, that makes me admire him even more.

"Let's go shopping," I say, taking a discreet step backward, away from him, but keeping my gaze fixed on his. "Before I lose myself in those gray eyes and forget everything else."

Liam's brow furrows slightly, as if he doesn't understand.

"Shopping?" he asks. "We're going shopping? For what?"

I nod, squeezing his hand, amused with his cluelessness. "A new truck, for starters," I tell him. "After that, we'll decide what's next. Tools, or stuff for the house, or clothes, or whatever you need."

Liam shakes his head, "No, we don't need to…"

"Yeah, we do," I insist, grabbing his hand, pulling him along toward the door. "And I'm not taking no for an answer anymore. I have more money than I know what to do with. Even if you decide you hate the fuck out of me, I can get you started with this. Let me."

"Ugh," Liam groans. "Fucking fine. I'll take your gifts, I guess."

On the way out, I remove the key from the front door and press it into Liam's palm.

"That's yours," I say. "There's only one, so don't lose it."

Liam stops walking. Beau stops with him, waiting patiently. He studies the key, his expression grave. Finally, taking in a catching breath, his eyes go misty. He wipes the evidence of this unexpected emotional reaction away quickly, sniffing, then shoves the key into his jeans pocket.

"Come on, Beau," he says, stroking the dog's scruff affectionately, while a reluctant smile brightens his usually serious expression. "Let's go shopping and see what that feels like."

CHAPTER SIX

LIAM

I don't know what to make of the last few hours. From the gleaming stone countertops in the kitchen of the caretaker's house to the way Beau ran around the place, sniffing every rug and chair, his tail wagging like he knew we were home before the word was ever spoken aloud. This day may be the most consequential in my entire life, rivaling the day I signed with Virginia Tech to play college ball. After that day, everyone treated me differently. I walked taller and stood broader with more confidence. I made eye contact without feeling inadequate. People spoke to me respectfully. It was the first time in my whole life I was treated like I mattered. I wasn't invisible anymore.

And right now, for the first time in so many years, I'm not invisible again.

"She's got a Vortec variable valve timing V8 engine that's E85 compatible," the car salesman says to me, gazing proudly on the truck idling in front of us. The salesman is six feet tall, and just about as big around, with a pork-belly bursting the buttons of his short-sleeved dress shirt that's pinned with a red plastic name tag identifying him as 'Big Bob.' I wonder silently to myself if there's a 'Little Bob' lurking around somewhere extolling the virtues of a smart red convertible.

"These FlexFuel engines can run on unleaded up to 85% ethanol, which gives you options, even with three hundred eighty foot-pounds of pulling torque. You can haul a whole damn house down the road with this thing."

If the house is on wheels and the road is headed downhill. Still, it's a very nice truck.

"You look like a tech-savvy type feller," he goes on, not quite sure when to quit selling and close the deal. "Did you see the touch screen entertainment system that's standard on this model? It's a Wi-Fi hotspot all on its own. You can stream movies, or listen to Sirius Satellite Radio, or your own music from Amazon, or even from MP3s stored on your phone."

I nod, glancing sideways at Grayson who's grinning at me from the sidelines. On the way over, he told me to be bold. He said to get the truck I want, not the truck I think I should settle for because I'm not paying for it. He reminded me that he's twenty seven years old and listed at number seventeen on the Forbes list of wealthiest Americans because he was lucky enough to convince the conmen on Wall Street that batteries were sexy.

"It's not even really my money," he says, shrugging. "It's not even really money at all until you spend it on something cool, that makes you happy, or that at least serves a purpose. Before that, it's just random digits in an account in some-body's database."

This truck I'm looking at, despite the fact that it's bright red, loaded with shit I don't need, and chromed to the Nth degree, is also an excellent work truck for the job Grayson's got in mind for me. It's a pickup with lots of clearance and hauling power. It's an office on wheels. It's perfect.

"He'll take it," Grayson says, coming up behind me, beating me to the punch.

I laugh. "You are *way* too much."

"So I've been told." He looks at his watch, then at the salesman, and hands him a business card. "We've got some other stuff to do. This is my banker's info. Call him. He'll handle the cash transfer. Just give me a call when it's ready to pick up. Okay?"

The salesman takes the card, scrutinizing the info on it carefully. He looks up, a question in his eyes. "California?" he asks. "Mountain View? What's SVB?"

Grayson nods, smiling patiently. "Silicon Valley Bank is a private bank for a fairly exclusive clientele. Call that number. Use my name. They'll arrange everything, I promise," he says. "In the meantime, we have things we need to do."

I almost hate leaving the big red pickup at the dealership, but Grayson's exuberance for our mission is contagious. Beau and I pile back into his car for the next stop on our journey, which is the mall in Bristol (since Abingdon's not big enough to have one).

I've never bought sheets before, or a comforter, or towels or washcloths for a bathroom. I never owned my own coffee pot before this shopping trip. I had part of my own bed when I was back in foster care, and I slept on top of my mattress with a thin comforter in college. Before everything went downhill.

"You need this," Grayson says, pointing to a fancy teak wood dish rack. "I have one at my place in Mountain View. It's nice."

It may be nice, but it's sixty-five dollars and the plastic one is only ten. That, and I don't actually own any dishes. I point out this fact to my benefactor.

"We need to fix that then," Grayson laughs, bee-lining to

the aisle where dinnerware sets are displayed like museum exhibits. "Come look at this! It's cool!"

Conspicuous consumption has never been my thing. I was raised in a succession of foster homes, bouncing from trailer park to rental house and back again. I know how to pillage a Goodwill, but shopping at the mall is a skillset I never mastered.

"Can we haggle the prices?" I ask Grayson while eyeing the tags doubtfully. "This shit's expensive."

Grayson leans sideways, checking the label on the dinnerware set he's considering on my behalf.

"It's not," he says. "It's not even two hundred dollars. Relax."

Two hundred dollars for plates? Is he smoking crack?

The mall sales staff was never happier to see any pair of queer shoppers cross their threshold. We buy damn near everything—one of each from almost every department. Grayson plops down his black Amex without batting an eyelash. To him, money is an existential concept. It's not quite real. It's only there for his entertainment.

To me, this is just surreal.

"Last stop," Grayson says, forcing his trunk closed. The back seat is crammed with shopping bags from floor to ceiling. It's so tightly packed there's no way to see out of the rearview mirror. Beau's going to wind up sitting in my lap. "We're going to Home Depot to get your tools."

It's getting late and getting dark. I'm hungry. Beau must be too, and there's no more room in the car for anything.

Grayson grins at me. "Or I could just give you my card and let you do that yourself tomorrow."

I nod, agreeing. This is his party and he's enjoying himself, but it takes energy to function in the shopping mall world. I haven't interacted with that many people or been so inundated with modern civilization in a long time. I spend most of my time alone trying to get by on whatever I can scrounge from other people's leavings. Today I used mental muscles that have been too long neglected.

"Let's get some dinner," Grayson suggests. "Take it home. Chill out and watch a movie – *or something.*"

Grayson makes me laugh with his not so subtle emphasis on 'or something'. We both know exactly what he's got in mind. Since I haven't seen an actual movie in years, I venture good natured negotiations.

"How about we watch a movie *and something,*" I say, climbing into the car, urging Beau to curl up in the snug space at my feet.

Grayson gets in, turns the ignition, checks his sideview, then pulls out. "I like that idea," he says, taking in a deep, satisfied breath. Biting his lip, he glances sideways at me. "I'm really glad I found you. I know this is all kind of crazy, but it… it feels right."

"It's weird… but it does feel right."

It does feel right, even though it also feels strange. It's like the last ten years evaporated into the ether, it's just me and Grayson again, and no time at all has passed. He's still the same as he was in school: slightly goofy, but so sweet and so generous. He was cute then. He's grown up to be gorgeous in that boy-next-door-billionaire way. He fills out his expensive, designer jeans in a way that's damn near obscene, and I can't help but keep looking at him.

Despite all that though, I know people are going to talk. I can handle the savaging, but Grayson's so sweet and probably naive about these things. I worry about how it's going to impact him and how he feels about this – about us.

He slips his hand around my knee. "Do you need anything from your truck before we go home?"

'Home.' The sound of the word is foreign to me. It's also the most beautiful sounding word I know of.

"Beau's dog food," I say. "And a change of clothes."

On the way back to Abingdon we pick up Chinese take-out, which fills the crowded car with the scent of good food, making my stomach growl. I can't wait to get 'home'.

My truck is parked behind the Bojangles Famous Chicken & Biscuits near the Walmart Supercenter. I like parking there because it's convenient to use the restrooms at Walmart, and Bojangles throws out a lot of food that's entirely edible. Every few hours they toss out fried chicken, biscuits, beans and rice, and anything that's been sitting around under the heat lamps longer than they consider reasonable.

My dumpster diving skills are at the top of their game, but that doesn't always make Bojangles' management happy.

When we pull into the fast food restaurant's parking lot and around to the rear where I've left my truck, I know instantly something's up. There's a big piece of yellow paper on my windshield tucked under my wiper blade. When we get closer, I spot a small white business card there with it. I know that combination and it isn't good.

"What's wrong?" Grayson asks.

I guess my posture changed, going on alert. Beau senses it too. He's up, trying to stand on his hind legs to see outside.

My ancient Toyota isn't classic enough to be cool. It's covered in dings and dents, its worst scrapes rusting through. The tires are going bald. Layers of grime make identifying the original color a challenge, but the engine is solid.

"That thing looks like shit," Grayson says. "It can't be safe to drive."

Safe is a relative thing.

Grayson parks beside my truck. When I open my door, Beau bounds out and bolts for the only 'home' he's ever known. He sleeps with me in the bed of the thing, the two of us curled up together, keeping each other warm. I take my meals on the open tailgate while feeding him at my feet.

"What's on the windshield?" Grayson asks.

It's a scrawled note from the manager of Bojangles threatening to tow my truck if I ever park it in his lot again, and threatening to charge me with trespassing if I ever go anywhere near their dumpsters again. The card is a business card from an Abingdon cop. There's a short note written in blue ink on the back. 'Move on,' it says. 'Call me if you have any questions.'

I hand the items to Grayson for his edification. "I'd have starved this year if it weren't for the perfectly good food this place throws away."

Grayson looks at the notes, then at the front door of the restaurant, then back at me. His expression turns angry.

"Fuck them," he says. "I'll buy the fucking franchise and change the corporate policy on leftovers. Why don't they donate it to the food bank or something?"

I shrug, shaking my head. "No clue," I tell him. "But I do know one thing. I need to move my truck, and…"

"Just follow me back home," Grayson says. "You can clean it out there, saving whatever you need, then we'll call a salvage company to come get it."

A salvage company? That ideas pricks my brain. It hadn't dawned on me until just now that I should let go of the Toyota. The thought of it grips me low in the gut, pulling hard at an empty space. This old truck has provided safety and shelter through blizzards and downpours, shade against a relentless summer sun, and a means of making a buck whenever I got an opportunity.

"Hey!" a voice calls from behind us. "You! Is that your truck!?"

Grayson and I turn in unison, facing a burly man coming toward us wearing brown polyester pants and an orange, white, and brown striped polyester shirt. There's a folded paper cap on his head and an apron hung around his neck, tied loosely behind his back. He's dusted head to toe in flour, spattered with grease and batter.

I feel my ire rise. This guy's about to pick a fight.

"It's mine," I say, squaring up. Beau instantly comes to my side, standing at the ready to get my back.

"You can't park it here!" the man barks, stopping short three feet away from me, his fists falling to his wide hips. "People think we're encouraging homeless people to loiter here. They see you. They complain. They worry about their kids and crime. It looks bad."

"Did you just accuse me of being a child predator and a thief?" I ask coolly. "If you did, we have a problem."

The man pauses, sizing me up, his eyes coming to the realization of what I already know: that I'd be more than capable of stomping his face into the concrete if he gave me half a reason.

Of course, if I did that, I'd only confirm his accusations. It's a dilemma.

"Only repeating concerns expressed by our customers," he says, dialing back his tone. "We just need you to move along."

"Your customers are ignorant white trash," I spit at him, pulling my keys from my pocket, feeling my blood rise hot in my chest. "And one paycheck away from living just like I do. Just like you."

"Liam, come on," Grayson says, placing his hand on my elbow. "You don't have to listen to this shit. You're done with this. Forever."

If I honestly believed I was done with this, I could laugh at the spattered man in front of me. Because I can't believe my delivery from homelessness and danger is entirely legitimate, I'm inclined to anger at every perceived insult. It's the first time all day someone has reminded me just how fragile my sense of self is. People look at me and they see a creep. They never bother to look any deeper than their own fears and perceptions.

I stare at the man and I want to hurt him. I want him to feel the sting of shame and humiliation I feel every single day of my life.

"Come on," Grayson says again. "While the egg rolls and crispy duck are still hot."

Crispy fried duck sounds at least six times better than Bojangles fried chicken. I don't ever have to eat Bojangles again if I don't want to. Or so Grayson keeps telling me.

I take a cautious step back towards my truck, glancing at Grayson. "I'll follow you." I say. "I know the way if we get separated."

He nods, moving toward his car, both of us leaving the restaurant manager standing idly in the parking lot watching us go. Beau hops into the cab ahead of me, taking his place on the passenger side, never taking his eyes off the dusty man. As we pass him in his polyester uniform, Beau gives him a low growl before turning his attention to the road ahead. Once we're cruising easy down Highway 58, following a few hundred feet behind Grayson, Beau settles down, dropping his head into my lap, closing his eyes.

He's had a big day and is thoroughly worn out. So am I. But inside, my guts churn, poisoned with a touch of lingering venom for that asshole fast food restaurant manager and his customers' judgement. I don't wish ill on anyone, but sometimes I do wish they could all walk in my shoes for just one day. Maybe then they wouldn't be so quick to cast aspersions or turn away. Maybe then there would be solutions to situations like mine, instead of just piling on the blame and the shame.

CHAPTER SEVEN

GRAYSON

*I*t's disturbing to experience firsthand the callous disregard with which Liam is treated by people who possess less than a fleeting fraction of his brains or his abilities. As angry as it makes me, I know I need to be chill for Liam's sake. I don't want to give encounters like that any more energy than they already command.

Henceforth, I'm making it my personal mission to make sure nobody ever talks to Liam like that again.

I watch his headlights in my rearview. I know he's in his truck with his best friend Beau, quietly seething about what happened. Seething -even though we had a fun day at the Chevy dealer buying a big, red pickup truck, then at the mall outfitting Liam's new cottage. It'll take a while for him to get his head wrapped around the idea that he's no longer home-less and he doesn't ever need to take anyone's shit. Money – or even the close proximity to money – is liberating like that. In time, I know he'll figure it out. I hope I can help speed the process along. I'm sure looking forward to trying.

* * *

BEAU RUNS into the mud room ahead of us. It's obvious he recalls being here and remembers his way around. He mounts the low stone steps up into the kitchen and finds his spot under the little desk by the pantry where he curls up, keeping his head up and alert, never taking his eyes off Liam.

"I need to feed him before anything," Liam says, dropping a bag of dry dog food on the counter with a thud. He produces a can, a spoon, and a steel bowl from the backpack he brought in from his old truck. At the sight of these things, Beau's tail wags violently, thumping hard on the floor.

Liam looks exhausted. He's got dark, drawn circles under his eyes and his shoulders are slumped with fatigue. He's also a bit ripe to the olfactory senses. I hadn't noticed it before, so I'm guessing the scene with the fast food manager sent him into an anxiety sweat; they're always pungent.

I reach forward, circling my palm behind Liam's head, drawing his gaze to mine. "Feed Beau," I say, peering into his perfect gray eyes. "Then go take a shower upstairs in my room. I've got drawers and closets full of clothes up there. Help yourself."

Liam shakes his head, pointing into his backpack. "I've got clothes," he says.

I peek inside, taking a deep whiff. The contents of that backpack smell of mildew and dog.

"No," I tell him. "No discussion."

I reach into the bag, pulling the musty t-shirt and laundry gray shorts, socks, and ripped jeans from within.

"These are going in the trash. Tomorrow when you take my card for a walk, you can walk it back to the mall to buy some new clothes."

Liam peers down at the pile of his clothes I've dropped on the counter beside Beau's dog food. Then his gaze moves back to me. This time his consideration falls to my clothing, starting low at my feet, working his way up, cataloguing my entire wardrobe.

His expression seems hurt.

"I'm not sure…" he begins. "I'm not sure I'd even know what to buy."

Liam never was much of a clothes horse. He was always poor, always wearing hand-me-downs. That only changed when he was at Virginia Tech, but then he dressed exclusively in clothes the team's sponsors provided.

"Okay," I say, testing the waters. "Would you like help?"

His eyes narrow. "What do you mean?"

I smile, resisting the urge to pet him like a plaything I've just fallen into passion with. "Your options range from me tagging along and offering suggestions, to hiring a personal stylist and shopper. Or I could probably solicit my sister or some friends…"

Liam shakes his head. "Do you have time? I don't want strange people…"

I can't help myself. I go up on my tip toes, quickly stealing a wet smooch. "Of course, I have time! If I didn't, I'd make time," I promise him, licking my lips, enjoying the taste of his. "Nothing I'd love better than helping you outfit that gorgeous body in something worthy of you. Now, feed Beau and go get a shower so we can eat."

Liam looks surprised, then amused. I made him happy. I cleared the doubting cobwebs from his mind. I showed him it's not the clothes that make the man, but the man himself I make room for. He'd make any clothes look good, but he deserves to feel confident in what he wears. He deserves to look fantastic.

He's gone a long time, showering by himself while I dish up our dinner, popping the covered plates in the oven to keep them warm. While I wait for Liam, I search streaming movies to watch while we eat. There's not much new, but when Liam comes in with wet hair, wearing just a pair of my PJ bottoms and a thin white undershirt, with Beau trailing at his heel, he spies the list of available films queued up on the screen and immediately gets excited.

"I saw a poster for this," he chirps. "And the music is great. Can we watch this one?"

"Of course," I tell him, handing him a plate of crispy fried duck, vegetable fried rice, crab rangoon, and a bowl of egg drop soup. "We can watch anything you want to see."

His selection is 'A Star is Born' starring Bradley Cooper (be still my heart) and Lady Gaga (already stole my heart). It won a Grammy, an Oscar, and a BAFTA, so I guess Liam's got decent taste in films. Somehow, I just didn't expect him to go for the sappy, romantic love story.

We watch the opening credits and first few scenes while we eat, with Liam wolfing down his dinner like a starving man. Before I know it, he's done and putting his plate aside. I grab a few more bites, then put mine aside too, settling in for the film just as we get to see Lady Gaga show off her raw talent.

"I love Gaga," Liam states, stretching out on the couch, resting his head in my lap as the story unfolds. "Gaga's gotten me through some shit."

He continues to surprise me. I reach down to his head, stroking soft, corn silk locks with adoring fingers. For so many years all I could do was think about Liam – *the one who got away* – and fantasize about moments like this that we never got to have. Liam's goodness and his affectionate touches back in high school ruined me for anyone other than him. We were so young, but I was old enough to love him, even if he didn't love me.

"Honey, Gaga's gotten a lot of people through a lot of shit," I quip, settling into the cushions, getting comfortable. "And she's gone through plenty herself."

"True facts," Liam says. He smiles.

The movie is beautiful and emotional, and it's inspiring. The story is the most classic tale in the world retold with a novel approach and nuanced attention to contemporary culture. There's intense drama and powerful performances, all of which combine to have me wrenched into tears by the time the film's climax arrives, but none of that is enough to keep Liam conscious.

Liam dozed ten minutes into the film. Thirty minutes and he's sound asleep, breathing deep and regular, his eyelids fluttering through a dream. While I watch the film, he turns in his sleep, rolling in my lap to face my belly. His hand slips around my waist, hugging me tight.

I let him sleep until the credits run, then I turn off the television and wait for silence to overtake the room. Once the soaring soundtrack of *A Star is Born* goes still, the creaking and settling of the old house are the only sounds audible; that and Liam's breathing.

A moment is all it takes to rouse him from his slumber. He startles awake, eyes opening wide, blinking, his body going rigid under my hand.

He looks side to side before moving, as if trying to piece together where he is and who he's with. Then, like an incoming tide, I watch the awareness flow in, settling him, softening his posture. He closes his eyes again, relaxing, his hand stroking the small of my back.

"Hey," he mumbles dreamily. "What did I miss?"

There's a tiny smile turning the corner of his lip.

"Everything," I whisper, resting a hand on his shoulder. "But I think you needed the rest."

He nods, smiling now, bringing his free hand up to my belly, lifting his index finger to touch the roll of flesh at my belly button. I'm wearing a t-shirt, but he easily slips his fingers under its hem, gently grazing my skin, sending a wave of electric pleasure straight down to my groin.

My cock responds instantly, firming up under Liam's resting head. He grins, rolling a few short strands of hair in his fingers.

"Let's go to bed," he purrs, blinking up at me through thick lashes. "But not to sleep. Not yet."

This time is completely different than the first time we were together. There's nothing to prove and nothing to be afraid of. It feels more genuine.

"Come here," he whispers, pulling me down with him onto the bed. "God, you feel good on me."

I do feel good on him. With our legs tangled together, our hips meeting, bellies pressed tight, I hover over him, waiting for him to tell me what to do. I'm almost afraid to move, lest I make him bolt again like he did the last time we were intimate.

"Don't run away in the morning," I tell him, dropping down to press lips to his after I say it. I taste his lips and tongue, sucking his heated breath into my hungry lungs. "You're a flight risk, Liam Gold, but I need you to hang on with me."

He nods, his eyes narrow, lids hooded, hungry with lust. His cock grows firm and tight against my leg.

"I won't go," he whispers. "Not 'til you want me to go."

I'd argue with him on his presumption that I'll ever want him to go, but Liam prevents me from arguing anything. My distraction is complete when he hooks a thumb around the waistband of my pajama bottoms and yanks them down, exposing my ass to the four walls. His hand reaches in low between us. In one quick move he's got both our cocks in hand, stroking them together. My brain fails me. I'm lost in how perfect this feels and the focused gaze Liam fixes me in as he makes my body into his plaything.

I've been with plenty men, but no one's ever touched me with such raw, sensuous physicality. He makes love like he used to play football: with an almost reckless joy that's completely contagious and absolutely intoxicating.

Each inconvenient position and offensive scent becomes a challenge for us to master and then defeat. We laugh through the awkward moments, letting the tension dissipate into an acceptance that this is what *real* sex is supposed to be: messy and crude, rough and easy in turns, hard work, and absolute bliss.

Our bodies fit like they were made for one another. As far as I'm concerned, there's not another body in the world that's even remotely interesting to me anymore.

"Oh fuck!" I cry, drawn up on my hands and knees on the sweat-drenched sheets with Liam's cock driving in so deep it tickles my tonsils. "Oh fuck!"

He's about to let go as I come hard, hot, and wet with sticky threads of jizz splattering between my knees, rippling down my inner thighs, dripping with molten heat.

A second later Liam explodes, pumping his full load of pent-up cum into me. The fingers of his right hand grip tight at my hip. His belly slams against the small of my back. His left hand grips my left shoulder, drawing me down against him.

He cries out when he comes, both hands squeezing me painfully.

A few expletives later (from both of us) and we collapse into a heaving heap on the soaked, sticky sheets, lungs begging for air, hearts racing.

"Fuck," Liam breathes. "Fuck, fuck, fuck."

I can't move. I'm a wreck. My head is a muddle. I don't even know what this is except... *It's perfect. I love it. I want more. I want it all.*

Without thinking, I roll over, turning toward Liam, scoop

him into my arms, and pull him close into my chest. His head rests on my breast, his ear pressed to the skin above my heart. I enclose him in an embrace, my lips pressed to the top of his head.

It's then that I see tears streaming down his cheeks. His eyes are closed, seared shut against the room, this world, against me. He swallows, driving back more tears, denying them air.

I tighten my grip, pulling him even closer into me.

"You're mine," I whisper above his ear. "And I'm yours. And you're safe no matter what comes. No matter what."

Liam's breathing settles quickly. A few moments later and he's slipped off to an easy sleep inside my arms. I caress his hair and very gently touch his cheek with the backs of my fingers, admiring his beautiful features, grateful for the fact that he can sleep easy with me.

"I love you so much," I whisper. "I always have, since we were kids. Baby, if I'd had any real idea how you were living, I would have done something, I swear. But now... *Now...* I promise you, you'll never be hungry or afraid again. You're safe, no matter what."

At our feet I hear a tentative whine and the click of claws on hardwoods. Beau lifts his head up, resting a heavy jowl on the foot of the bed. His sad, doleful eyes peer at me.

"Come on!" I urge him, patting an empty space beside us.

He leaps up on powerful hind legs, launching onto the king-sized mattress.

"Good boy!" I praise, stroking the loose skin between his ears and shoulders. Beau sniffs Liam, pausing to make sure he's breathing. Satisfied, he turns twice then drops into a circle of dog perfection at our feet.

I slide under the covers, drawing my arms around Liam, snugging him into me.

"I love you," I mumble into his ear, breathing deep.

A few minutes later, I drift away into bliss. I'm wrapped up in my dreams and in the scent and flesh of my dream come true.

I've accomplished a lot in my life, but winding up with Liam Gold sleeping peacefully inside my embrace might just be my greatest achievement to date.

CHAPTER EIGHT

LIAM

his might be what it feels like to win the Mega-Millions Powerball Lottery. It's like the core of the Earth shifted under my feet and now everything's topsy-turvy.

Last week I was homeless, broke, hungry, out of options, and – aside from Beau – completely alone. This week I've got a nice place of my own, a job that pays ridiculously well, crispy duck leftovers in the fridge, and time and money to go shopping for anything I need. I also have Grayson Ellis hunched between my thighs, his sweet lips wrapped around my cock, sucking, slurping, swirling his tongue in such profoundly creative ways. He's grinning through it while I moan, too, trying my best not to come. He's loving every minute of this. So am I.

Aside from being a carefree billionaire, the thing that's most attractive about him is the fact that he's so into this and doesn't give a rat's ass what anyone else thinks of him. He revels in it – in me – sucking up every drop of me I can give him.

He woke me up this morning with his mouth doing things to my body I've scarcely imagined before.

"Oh, God, Grayson," I huff, slipping my hands around the sides of his head, fingers lacing through thick, straight hair. "I can't hold it anymore."

He grins with my cock swallowed deep in his throat. Then – with the point of his tongue made sharp and rigid – he traces a line, hot and fast, around the base of my glans, sending me into the orgasm stratosphere. My brain explodes in a shower of blinding technicolor. My ears play a symphony in perfect synchrony with the pulsing rhythm of wave after wave of pleasure pouring into and out of my entire body.

For a few blissful seconds I'm lost in a sea tide of warm, wet, bliss; every cell in my body is animated by Grayson's attentions.

When I'm finally semi-conscious again, I peer down between my legs at Grayson. He's looking up at me, eyes wide, smiling. His pink lips are swollen, a glistening drop of my essence at the corner of his mouth. He's licking his lips like he likes my taste.

I'm about to say something either profound or profoundly stupid, when Beau jumps up from his napping perch on the floor and runs toward the window, barking loud. He hops up, placing front feet on the sills so he can see out. Once he sees what's beyond the window, he turns on the watchdog role like he's trying hard to earn his keep. He's barking and growling like he intends to kill and eat whatever is out there.

Way to kill a mood.

"What in the hell..." I freeze—whenever Beau does this, it's because of some kind of danger. Or law enforcement getting me to move my car. My heart sinks, and there's a flutter of anxiety deep in my core.

Grayson puts his hand on mine and examines my face. "Hey, Liam. It's okay."

"Yeah, yeah." I swallow hard. "Of course it is."

Grayson takes my fingers and kisses them, sending a reassuring warmth through my veins.

But I'm still paralyzed. Grayson gathers his energy, popping up with alacrity. He damn near glides to the window, pulling the curtain aside as if he doesn't care who sees him stark naked.

"Shit," he says, turning back to me with a surprised grin. "Your tools are here!"

Grayson throws on a white linen shirt and faded khaki cargo shorts. He doesn't bother with shoes.

* * *

THREE GRUFF GUYS and a delivery truck from Lowes Home Improvement, carrying a bunch of high-end equipment—table saws, circular saws, nail guns, a really nice band saw, and every possible hand and battery-operated power tool Grayson's money could buy. They're moving all of it out into the driveway, and Grayson is animatedly telling them where to put it and how quickly. He's *beaming*.

Just as I appear downstairs in bare feet, pulling on a shirt, one of the guys rolls a huge Craftsman tool cabinet down a ramp off the back of the truck. It's five feet tall and rolling on casters, still wrapped in shrink wrap to keep the drawers closed.

"Where should we put this stuff?" One of the workers looks to me, since Grayson clearly has no idea—he's been paying people to figure shit out for him for so long now that he hasn't had to worry about setting up a business or making any home repairs by himself. Hell, the whole house has probably been set by the most expensive decorator in Virginia.

Grayson hands me a cup of coffee with a smile. "You're on your own. There are three separate sheds and a... five car garage, I think," he says, batting long eyelashes, adorable with his sex-tousled hair. "You can set up wherever you want."

I laugh, in spite of myself. This is an insane display of materialism—and worth more money than I've ever had in my life. But Grayson's enthusiasm is absolutely contagious, and for once, I let myself feel the same. "This way," I direct the delivery crew.

There's a wide screened-in porch near the driveway that's safe from blowing rain and burning sun that is also out of the way of foot traffic. I spied it a day or two ago, thinking to myself it wouldn't be a bad workshop. It's a large open space where I can get a lot of work done building cabinets and cutting new trim without having Grayson or any of his staff tripping over me. It's also a recent addition to the house, so if I manage to screw up the floors or set something on fire, it's no biggie. I plan on tearing down the thing eventually and restoring the portico that was original to the house.

"Just put it all right in here," I show them. "Leave it all in boxes. I'll unpack everything and set it up."

"Are you sure?" one of the men ask. "We can uncrate the big stuff for you."

I shake my head, grinning like a kid at Christmas. "I'll do it," I tell him. "That's half the fun of it. Just stack everything up in the middle of the floor here."

The delivery guys are still hauling boxes off the truck when a car appears up the driveway, crawling slowly toward the house. It's a cobalt blue Thunderbird coupe with tinted glass. I'd know that car anywhere. It's Grayson's sister, Melanie Ellis. She came back to Abingdon four months ago and opened an art gallery, instantly catapulting to A-lister status, alongside Nikki Rippon, Zane Chase, and Kendall Vincent. A month after that, her boyfriend showed up. They started throwing parties and making themselves indispensable. I got hired to haul trash after one of their soirées. They didn't pay very well. I doubt she remembers me, but just in case, I'm going to try to lay low.

"Where do you want this, Mr. Gold?" a grizzled delivery man asks me, holding a heavy box filled with bandsaw components.

"In the corner," I tell him, pointing, following him into the shadows of the screened porch.

I watch Melanie park her car. Getting out, she peers curiously at the Lowes truck and the activity going on within. She moves toward the main part of the house and to her brother who is probably on his second cup of coffee already making calls to California.

I think I'm in the clear, having successfully avoided any scrutinizing contact with the potentially judgmental world of Grayson Ellis's family members, when I'm proved woefully wrong. I'm sending the delivery guys off with a handshake and signed papers when another car appears, this one tearing down the gravel drive, kicking up dust and rocks rather than crawling slowly. The car—an Audi with a rental plate and a Hertz window sticker—grinds to a halt ten paces from the Lowes truck. The driver's side door pops open as I'm about to walk away, and a guy—a big guy with chocolate colored hair and a square head—steps up and out, his eyes fixed on me.

"What's all this?" he asks me, as if I'm obliged to respond.

I pause, peering over my shoulder at him, taking him in. "Excuse me?" I ask.

He looks me up and down. Something in his demeanor tells me he disapproves of what he sees. There's a smirk on his face, one that shows me exactly who this person is. The high school quarterback, the bully, the guy who takes pleasure in picking on other people.

"What's the truck delivering?" he asks, cocking his head to the side like he belongs here and I do not. "And who are you?"

Oh, he can go straight away and fuck himself.

"Talk to Grayson." I say, turning to walk away, doing my best to dismiss him entirely.

"I'm talking to *you*," he snaps, his tone sharp and condescending. "What are you doing here?"

I'm just about five seconds away from telling him that an hour ago I was balls deep up Grayson's pristine, tight ass— which is just about six times better than I fantasized in high school—when Grayson himself appears with his sister on his arm.

Grayson and Melanie stroll up just in time to keep me from calling out this douche. Grayson's eyes smile like he knows what I'm about.

"This is my sister, Mel," he says calmly, a bemused smile creasing his pretty blue eyes. "Mel, this is Liam. You remember him from high school?"

She gives me a big toothy grin, smiling warmly like she's known me for years. "I remember your touchdowns and the speeches you gave at pep rallies. I was too young to talk to you back then. I was in ninth grade at Abingdon High when you were a senior at Jackson."

And still, she remembers me. *Amazing.*

"What's all this?" the guy asks again, directing his inquiry to Grayson. "Who is this guy?"

Grayson lets his eyes flow to the man inquiring about me. He gives the man a patient, almost sympathetic expression.

"Tony Carraro, this is Liam Gold," Grayson says, smiling at me, not letting go of his sister's arm. "We've been friends since we were in ninth grade or something ridiculous like that. Since forever. Liam, this is Tony, our COO at Theos."

"COO?" I ask. "What is that exactly?"

The square headed man with chocolate colored hair glares at me. "Chief Operations Officer," he barks. "That's everything from security to branding. It's a wide scope."

I can't help but smile. "Jack of all trades," I observe, not finishing the cliché. *Master of none.* And clearly a total douche. "We have that much in common. I do a little of this and a little of that. Grayson hired me to handle the renovation on the house here, so I'll be honing my restoration carpentry skills."

Tony appears briefly confused, then he regards Grayson with question. "You don't usually get personally involved with menial tasks like hiring peripheral labor," he says. "You delegate that sort of thing."

'Menial tasks' and *'peripheral labor'*? Tony knows how to craft an insult while making the object of his jibe sound important.

Melanie clenches her jaw, her eyes darting to meet mine, then quickly looks away. She flushes a pretty hue of pale pink on my behalf.

"No, I don't," Grayson agrees, smiling coolly. "But I think from now on I'll take a lot more interest in what's going on here. My priorities have been way too focused on work and nothing else. I need to broaden my horizons."

"Amen! I'm so glad you said that," Melanie says, squeezing Grayson's arm tight against her ribs while Tony looks on, confounded. "You need to be here more. Get your hands dirty. You've been a one-trick pony for too long, Grayson. It's time you learned to do something useful, like how to build something or how to talk to people."

"Yeah," Tony says. "Except Grayson has a company to run, a few thousand employees depending on him, and a bigger bottom line than some developing nations. He doesn't exactly have time for woodworking hobbies."

Grayson lets go of Melanie's hand. He locks eyes with Tony, giving him a deliberately confrontational expression.

"I'll *make* time," he says, his voice low and steady. "Just like you make time to be here. You should really be back in Mountain View watching over the company instead of here, worried about how I spend my down time. I feel like I'm *your hobby*, Tony. Why is that?"

"The board wanted me to check in with you, so they sent me out here. I was happy to oblige," Tony says, shrugging. "They're on edge. You leaving town doesn't help. They get nervous. That's all."

Grayson rolls his eyes, shaking Tony's response off dismissively. "Go home, Tony. Let me enjoy a few weeks off with family without having to worry about Theos. If the board is worried about me, then maybe they should listen to me more instead of blocking every progressive move I make."

Tony has no response. He just clenches his jaw, nodding and trying to look sympathetic.

"Go back to Mountain View," Grayson says again. "And tell the board to get the fuck out of my way and stop trying to kill my company."

"Technically, it's not your company," Tony says, hedging awkwardly, his tone anything but confident. "We're a publicly traded…"

"You test that theory," Grayson goads. "Go ahead. Tell the board to test it. Let's see who's right."

I can't decide if Tony is a stooge for some arch-enemy board of directors, or just a dumb fuck who likes to follow the boss around, attempting to engage him with shit that's clearly above his pay grade. Grayson appears to think it's the former, but Tony doesn't seem bright enough for a board of directors to charge him with such an important job.

84

What is the board nervous about? Why would they send Tony to check on Grayson?

Something shady must be going down. Grayson must have some scheme up his sleeve. He's always thinking six moves ahead. That's why he's who he is, and we're all 'the rest.' There's no way to beat him or anticipate him because he's already played every potential move out at least half a dozen ways before he takes a single step.

Whatever the board is worried about, their concerns are too little, too late. Their worst fears have already come to fruition.

Grayson Ellis is in Abingdon, and he's planning to stay.

CHAPTER NINE

GRAYSON

*E*ven though I told Tony to go home, he didn't immediately comply. He *needed* to meet with me in my Abingdon office, for whatever ridiculous reason he's thought up.

"What are you doing, Grayson?" Tony asks me, his tone loaded with genuine concern and judgment. "We've been together a long time. I know you better than anyone. I've never seen you acting like this."

I lean back in my chair, my long legs crossed, eyes fixed on Tony, taking him in in his entirety. Once upon a time, I found him handsome. There might have even been a time when I could have entertained having more than just a professional relationship with him. That was when I was young, overwhelmed with loneliness, and afraid of being alone. Tony — though he never intended to—taught me that it's better to be alone than to fill your life with vapid, meaningless relationships just for the sake of collecting the approval of strangers.

Tony's a collector of people. I'm possibly his prize specimen. He—like Theos's board of directors—doesn't want me to get away. He wants to exert some kind of control over me, and I'm not terribly fond of the idea. His entire presence makes me feel claustrophobic.

"How am I acting?" I ask him. *Happy?* Distracted by something that's not a new product launch? Unconcerned with fighting with the board? "Because I'm on vacation. It's not any of your business how I'm acting, Tony."

Tony nods, draws a chair near my desk, turns the back around, and climbs over it like he's mounting a horse or a Harley Davidson. (I've never quite been able to define what the heck Tony is overcompensating for, but I know there's something.)

"That's just it," he says, sitting forward, crossing his arms over the backrest of his mount. "You haven't ever taken a vacation before. Now, suddenly, you're gone for a week with no return date and instructions to your PA not to schedule anything for the foreseeable future. And you're renovating a house in Abingdon, Virginia of all places."

"It's where I grew up," I say tersely.

He glances through the open doorway to his left, straight into the shadows of my bedroom. His eyes fall to Liam's worn backpack and his jeans tossed over it, a pair of threadbare boxers dropped on like a cherry topping an ice cream sundae. "And then there's the guy downstairs," Tony observes, rocking his head side to side like he's just come upon something that smells funky. "The one who looks like a gigolo with bad tattoos."

I can't help but laugh. Though after I get past the humor, the comment makes me angry.

"I think you've crossed a line," I tell Tony. "My personal life – the people who I invite to drop their backpacks in my bedroom—is in no way relevant to what we're doing at Theos. Your curiosity about that particular topic reinforces my concerns that my life has been fully co-opted by the company. The company doesn't have a say in..."

"It does," Tony interrupts. "It does, and here's why."

He pushes off his chair mount, standing quickly, then turns on heel waving his arms wide with animated drama. "Grayson, you have seven thousand employees. We've got contracts in the billions, most of them federal. This company has rejuvenated the alternative energy industry in *this* country and is moving global economies. Everything you do —from what you have for breakfast in the morning to whose dick you suck—impacts stock prices, contract terms, and market shifts. You suck the *wrong* cock, and you could crash Wall Street in an afternoon."

Oh, good lord.

"Ridiculous," I snort. "You're being a little hyperbolic, aren't you?" I cross my arms, anger rising inside me and threatening to boil over.

"I don't know what that means," Tony replies. "But I do know that guy down there looks like the kind of parasite who attaches to wealthy, important people like you, gets some dirt on them, then drains them slowly for years, all while making them crazy. I don't want to see that happen to you, Grayson. I can handle him if you want me to. I'll do it right now."

Wow. The places Tony's mind goes. It's sad, really, when you realize just how cynical and mean so many people are.

"You're wrong," I say plainly. "You're just so very, very wrong."

I stand up, going to my personal files in a cabinet against the wall. I open a drawer, quickly locating the file I'm looking for. It's the private investigator's complete file on Liam, from the first day I engaged his help in locating him.

I hand the folder to Tony.

"Liam and I were best friends in high school," I tell him

again as he takes the folder in hand. "We lost touch after graduation. I've been looking for him for years. Trust me when I tell you, he's not a stalker or any kind of parasite. He's as dear to me as family, and there's nothing you can say or do to break that."

Tony's just about to protest, arguing the validity of my own feelings to me, when my phone rings, conveniently interrupting us.

The caller ID says it's a Boston number, so I have to guess it's someone from Nicolai Automotive, maybe even Justin Trivet.

"I've got to take this, Tony," I say. "If you'll excuse me. Also, book yourself a flight back to California."

Tony gives me a look, clutching the folder in his fist while glaring at my phone. "Who is it?" he asks, as if every aspect of my world is within his purview to inspect.

"Tony, go!" I say, pointing toward the threshold. "I'll be down in a few."

I back him out as he protests, closing my office door behind him, then retreat into my bedroom and close that door too. I don't want this conversation inadvertently overheard. It's far too important and much too sensitive for anything to leak out before the deal is done.

CHAPTER TEN

LIAM

My uncle, "Puck," was my mother's brother. He was the only living tie I had to any of my blood relations. He tried hard to keep me close, but he was in no position to take care of a kid on his own. He was a thirty-something gay guy trying to keep a small contracting business afloat in a conservative, mountain town in western Virginia. It was bad enough that he was gay, but the idea that his little sister came home pregnant after following some rock band around the country scandalized the already bad reputation my family earned over the decades.

My grandparents wanted no part of me. When I came online, they were just cozying up to the idea that they might get to retire with a few bucks free to play bingo or the lottery. The last thing they needed was a toddler bleeding them dry of time and treasure. My mother was even less interested in being a parent. She had her head focused on becoming a famous country music star. She left me with a woman from county family services and never even looked back as she walked away. Just a few days shy of my eighth birthday, she died alone in a Memphis hotel room with a needle hanging out of a blown vein. I didn't learn about it until months after it happened, when my uncle Puck came to my foster home to tell me.

By then I was already well-embedded in the system. When my mother died, my uncle felt bad for me. He couldn't take me in full time, but he didn't let me go either. He became my lodestone—my constant. The county would send me from one foster home to another, then put me in a group home for a while, then maybe in the state orphanage for a few months, again and again. But no matter what, Puck would show up to visit and take me out for a weekend when he could. When I got older, he'd take me for weeks on end so I could work with him and his contracting crew.

It was Puck who got the Stainbeck family in Abingdon to take me in. Mr. and Mrs. Stainbeck were one of those couples who always have a house filled with kids of every age, color, and persuasion. They owned a big, old rambling farmhouse and possessed a bottomless well of patience and yes, even love, for the kids who passed through their rooms over the years. With my uncle lobbying for me, they took me in when I was fifteen years old, about to enter ninth grade, and a genuine handful of hormones and rebellion.

I started out at the public school in Abingdon, but as soon as Jackson's head football coach, Bobby McGuiness, saw me play, it didn't take long for them to extend a scholarship offer. Kids in my situation don't question acts of generosity like that. We accepted the offer and I moved over to Jackson Academy in the spring of my freshman year. After that, everything else just fell into place—until it all blew up.

Gazing at this fancy new cabinet saw that was just delivered, I know my uncle Puck would have been envious. He had great tools, and he cared for them like they were his kids. When he got killed trying to break up a random bar fight in Bristol, I inherited his tools. I didn't have them long before someone broke into my truck and stole them all. That was a bleak day. Now, I think things may be looking up for the first time in a very long time.

It took me the better part of an hour to unpack the saw and get it situated in a spot where I can use it. Now, all I need to figure out are the accessories. With this thing, I can build new cabinets and built-in custom shelves for every room in the house. I can do fancy vanity doors and paneled wall coverings. There's no limit to what I can do.

I'm falling in love with my tools and ignoring everything else around me – including Beau's over-loud snores where he's curled up in the corner, sound asleep – when I hear the crunch of heavy tires on the gravel outside.

Coming around the corner, I spy the reason for my interruption and I'm glad for it.

The prettiest, fire-engine red, four wheel drive Hemi pickup with lots of chrome and a dual exhaust cruises up the drive trailed by a minivan bearing the logo wrap of the dealership in Abingdon. That's a sweet truck. It's hard to believe it's really mine—*sort of mine*, anyway.

Beau howls up at the sky, then looks at me like I've got some explaining to do.

The truck pulls up close. When the driver steps out, he's clearly diverted by the house and grounds and whatever story is wrapped around this truck he just delivered.

"I've got paperwork," he says cautiously, climbing down from the cockpit of the thing, a clipboard in his hand. "Are you Mr. Ellis or Mr. Gold?"

"Gold," I reply.

He shoves the clipboard in front of me, pointing toward a highlighted 'X'.

"Sign here," he instructs, giving me a curious look. "Nice truck. Congrats."

I sign as instructed. The man tears out a yellow colored

sheet from the carbon-copy stack I just signed and hands it to me.

"The title is in the glove box," he says, stashing his ball point pen behind his ear. "The plates are temporary. Your new ones should be in the mail within a week. The keys are in the ignition. What else can I do for you?"

I'm about to ask for a quick lesson on the built-in entertainment system when I'm interrupted by another unexpected appearance of Tony Carraro. Wasn't he supposed to go home?

"What the everloving fuck is this?" His tone is laden with wonder. "Grayson bought you a fucking truck?"

"Oh, look at that," I say coolly. "I had no idea you were still here. I thought Grayson told you to book a flight back to Mountain View."

The delivery man's brow knits tightly as he shifts his disapproving gaze between me and Tony. "If that's all, we'll be on our way," he says, taking a step back. "Call the office if you have any questions."

I guess I'll figure out the entertainment system on my own.

Tony takes a step toward me, his eyebrows knitted together and an ugly grimace covering his face. "You must think you just stumbled up on a winning lottery ticket or something," Tony says, glaring first at me, then at the truck. "But you didn't. You're just a piece of shit gold digger who won't hold Grayson's attention. You're a high school fantasy that he'll realize was better in his imagination than in reality. He'll figure that out. He's a smart guy."

Tony walks toward the truck, folding his arms across his chest, sucking in his cheeks.

"You're not even a creative gold digger," he observes, checking himself out in the truck's side mirror. "The dumb ones go for toys and vehicles. The smart ones go for investment grade securities and real estate. Guess which kind you are?"

I'm just about to get angry again, when I realize Tony is talking about himself as much as he is me. The hair, the clothes, the fancy car; they're all trappings whose exclusive purpose is to appeal to someone important to him... *to Grayson?*

"Is that what *you* get?" I ask him. "Investment grade securities? Do you get anything else? Like Grayson's affection in appreciation for all you do for him? Do you get enough? Or do you need more?"

Tony stops admiring his reflection, his eyes closing on mine, then narrowing. "Fuck you," he spits. "It's not like that. I work for Grayson, but *not* like you do."

I smirk. "I bet you'd like to though," I suggest, walking toward him. I stop just inside the perimeter of his personal space—showing him that I'm a solid three inches taller than he is. "Unfortunately, it's tough to compete with the kind of history Grayson and I have. There's nothing I wouldn't do for him. I don't care how it looks to you or to anyone else. All I care about is how Grayson feels. Trust me when I tell you, he feels pretty damn good."

Tony huffs, shaking his head. "You're smarter than you look," he hisses. "But Grayson's too smart to fall for your bullshit for long. He deserves better than you, and he'll figure that out."

"Are you what he deserves?" I ask him, my suppressed resentment simmering. "Is that why you're here? Am I in your way, Tony? Are you trying to get closer to the *boss*? Is that why you flew all the way across the country—to get Grayson back where you want him?"

Tony's jaw clenches. His face flushes crimson. He doesn't deny what I've said! He's blanking—at a total loss for words!

I grin, then laugh out loud. "Damn, talk about awkward!"

I exclaim. "You show up here out of the blue, and here I am with a prior claim."

Tony fumes. It's obvious I've touched a sensitive nerve. It's just as clear that he doesn't like being laughed at, which only makes me want to laugh even more.

"I bet it sucks, huh?" I ask, a teasing tone dripping off my tongue. "The idea that some broke-ass loser with bad knees is more Grayson's speed than... *you?*"

He's just about to blow a vein on the side of his head—such is his unvented rage—when he stops, takes a breath, and steps back.

"Cool!" Grayson says, walking up behind me. "They brought the truck!"

I smile, then wink at Tony, stepping back and circle into Grayson's outstretched arms.

"I hope you like it," he says, pulling me close, smiling at me, his eyes bright, happy.

I nod. "I love it," I tell him. Then I lean in, nuzzling, stealing a sweet, affectionate kiss as I hook my thumbs through his belt loops—pulling him even closer to me with a tender familiarity I haven't risked outside the bedroom before. "I didn't even realize how much until just now, when your friend Tony pointed out just how lucky I am that we found each other again. I'm the luckiest broke-ass loser with bad knees on the planet."

Grayson smiles, kissing me back, obviously pleased with my gesture. Then he shifts a questioning glance to Tony.

"Really?" he asks, clearly uneasy with the idea that Tony has had anything nice to say about our relationship. "Is that a fact?"

Tony scowls, rolling his eyes high to the heavens and back down, shoving his hands in his pockets. He shakes his head, his scowl deepening.

"Grayson, what do you think you're doing?" he asks, arms

falling to his sides, palms out, imploring. "Help me understand this."

Grayson's hand slips snugly around my waist, fingertips firm against my flesh. He takes a breath, his expression pensive. He nods at Tony, pursing his lips slightly.

"Life," Grayson replies, holding on to me. "I'm doing life. It isn't all about stock valuations and product launches. It isn't all about crushing the competition."

"Since when?" Tony asks, confusion marking his brow.

Grayson just laughs, shaking his head. He turns to me, grinning sideways. "Where's Beau? Let's go for a drive in the new ride, eh?"

I nod, whistling for Beau. He comes running, stopping short when he sees Tony. He drops his head, his tail straightening, a low, guttural growl rolling from within him.

Tony glares at Beau and then at me. "Enjoy yourself," he says to Grayson. "I'm at the Washington Inn when you're ready to do some work."

"I'm on vacation," Grayson reminds him. "You should try it sometime. It's great. Maybe you could drive down to Asheville. You know, *away* from here."

"I would love to," Tony says, exasperation shredding his tone. "But I've got a company to run since you're not so interested anymore."

"I'm interested," Grayson replies. "Just not to the absolute exclusion of everything else that matters."

"*This* matters?" Tony asks, gesturing toward me, to the red truck parked in the drive, then to the ridgeback dog still holding a defensive position against him. "This is what matters to you more than what we built?"

Grayson considers Tony's question. It's clear he knows his answer will make a statement he can't take back. It's clear he knows the statement he makes will have repercussions.

He smiles, nodding. "More than anything," he replies, his eyes brighter than ever. "More than anything in the world."

Tony is stunned. He looks hurt—perhaps crushed. Then he gathers himself. He shakes off everything he's heard and seen.

"You'll come to your senses," he says, frustration still evident in his tone. "I know you will. You're too smart to go down this path, and there's too much at stake. Get this shit out of your system. Do whatever you need to do."

Tony doesn't linger. He gets in his car and drives away as we watch. Grayson shrugs behind him as he goes.

I'm tempted to tell Grayson what I know—that Tony is *definitely* in love with him, or at least infatuated with the thought of being in love with him. I decide not to do it though, as I figure Grayson either already knows, or doesn't want to. Either way, I know Tony poses no genuine threat to us, but he still annoys me and I'll be glad when he's gone.

"Let's go for that drive," I say, taking Grayson's hand in mine, pressing his knuckles to my lips for a quick kiss. "Come on Beau!"

I have Tony to thank for one thing: he made me realize this brand new thing Grayson and I have—however surreal it feels to me—is something I'm ready to defend. Grayson was the best thing that happened to me when I was a kid of just fifteen, and he's still the best thing that's ever happened to me. I know at some point soon he's going to pack up and go back to his normal life in California, and I don't know what happens or how that's going to work, but I do know that I'm not letting go of him again—not without a fight.

CHAPTER ELEVEN

GRAYSON

J was never much of a driver. I've had a chauffeur for the past five years, and I don't drive in California unless I have to. It's beautiful there—I can't say that it's not. But there's something vastly different about Virginia's Blue Ridge Mountains, the soft, rolling mountains, a touch of gray haze on the skyline, cotton-candy clouds moving overhead.

We drive through the country for thirty miles or more, just testing Liam's new Silverado. The engine is quick and responsive, the turns easy and tight. Liam's hand rests on my thigh as we wind along back roads. Beau sits with me, his head in my lap, looking up at me with his wide brown eyes. There's classic country music on a scratchy FM station coming out of West Virginia, and the air is honey dew crisp, promising an early frost. I could get accustomed to a life like this.

I think Liam is settling in to the idea of being my boyfriend. He says so little, but when we're alone he isn't stingy with his affections. Just like his hand on my leg now: he's a little bit possessive—in the sexiest way possible. I've never been attracted to that quality. It always struck me as needy or even slightly creepy, but with Liam there's a sweetness about the way he reaches for me that just makes me melt into a puddle beside him. Nobody else has ever had that kind of effect on me.

I know Liam wasn't out in college. He was there on an athletic scholarship. Plenty of well-connected people would have made it difficult for him if he'd tried to express his authentic self. I don't know exactly what his social and sex life has been since recovering from his injury, but it's obvious he's not exactly clubbing it every weekend. And yet, he kissed me in front of Tony. Maybe he was just staking his turf (which I'm fine with, if that's all it was). Or maybe he's getting more comfortable being real (which would be even more awesome).

I need to take a leaf from that book and be my own authentic self. I'm guilty of lying—or at least omission of relevant fact—to Liam. I need to come clean and tell him why I'm hiding out in Abingdon, and why I can't stay much longer. It wasn't only that I needed a trip home. And I need to tell him about that soon.

We're almost home and I'm hungry, but the cupboard is bare.

"Head to town," I suggest. "We need to get something for dinner. What are you up for?"

Liam smiles casually. "Let's call in something and get it delivered," he says. "I'm ready to settle in for a quiet evening."

I didn't even know delivery was an option. As far as I know the best restaurant in town is the Tavern, a place I've been to a couple times with my sister. Once we're back home, we give the online menu a once-over. Then Liam calls in our order with pick-up and delivery instructions to an Uber driver he knows.

"Let's go hang out by the water while we wait," I suggest,

retrieving a bottle of wine from the cooler, wanting to enjoy this beautiful weather while it lasts. "I've got some stuff I need to share with you."

"Okay," he says, his voice cool.

I nod toward the cabinet. "Grab us a couple glasses."

Liam does as I ask, but his expression sharpens as if he dreads hearing inevitable bad news.

I take his free hand in mine. "Relax," I tell him, pressing my lips to his fingers. "What I need to tell you isn't bad. It's good."

The decking above the dock and boathouse is weathered and creaks underfoot, but it'll last a few more years before it needs to be ripped out and replaced. We sit at a rough-hewn farm table and chairs under a cantilevered roof, high on a bluff overlooking the lake. The water is flat and green, reflecting the sky and the few evening clouds floating by overhead. When the sun goes down behind us, the water will shade to black as the sky darkens, making a bit of an optical illusion of starry sky above and below the horizon. That's my favorite view of the lake.

I pour both of us a glass of wine. Liam is quiet, regarding me pensively. He knows something is coming. Beau sits at his feet, gazing up at his dad like Liam is the master of the universe. He may just be.

I lean back against the deck railing, peering over my shoulder across the lake to the north side where a boat landing floats on the lake's surface. A decade ago, at that exact spot, there were only trees and fallen logs at the water-line a few dozen yards from a secluded parking lot in the woods.

"You remember when we used to sit over there and dream about this place?" I ask Liam.

He nods, taking a sip from his glass. "I sure do," he says.

"I told you one day I was gonna buy this place for you," I

hesitate, realizing this may all be too fast, terrified of scaring him off. A chill lifts between my shoulder blades, freezing my brain. "Anyway..." I stammer inexplicably. *No one makes me this self-conscious!* "I've got some things I need to talk about."

Liam—sensing my discomfort—doesn't get in my way. He waits patiently for me to select the necessary words.

"I'm... I'm selling Theos," I finally spit out. "That's why I'm here in Abingdon, straggling and laying low, rather than in Mountain View or anywhere else. I'm afraid news is going to leak and I'm just trying to create plausible deniability until the deal is done. I don't want anyone to know about this."

Liam's eyes narrow. "Why are you selling?" he asks, obviously surprised. "And why is it such a big deal?"

I take a larger than normal gulp of wine, hoping it will chill me out.

"I'm burnt out," I admit, saying it aloud for the first time. "I've done nothing but eat, sleep, dream, and exist for that company since day one. Now that it's up and going, I just want out. I'm done. I can't give it any more of my good years."

Liam's expression is loaded with unspoken question, but he says nothing. I need to explain myself more completely.

"I'm taking my life back," I say, placing my hand on his knee. "I bought the lake house thinking I could reclaim some kind of roots in Abingdon. I hoped... *maybe*... that I could make a different life than I've had so far."

Why is this so hard? Liam's looking at me like I'm speaking in a foreign tongue.

"I think you're a big part of that better life I'm plotting for myself," I say. "If you're okay with being in my life, I want you to be. It was a coincidence that I found you here. But this is what I've wanted... for years. Forever, I think. Life is short. I've been realizing it more and more."

Initially, he doesn't say anything. That scares me to death, thinking I've said way too much way too fast. He looks stunned or perhaps puzzled. Finally, he speaks.

"I'm more than okay being in your life," he says, slipping his fingers around mine where they still rest on his knee. "You're just as fascinating to me now as you were all those years ago. But I've already told you I'm not cultured, and I'm not wealthy. I don't have the same background that you do. I know you'll lose interest—"

I start shaking my head before he can finish the sentence.

"... I'm willing to try to hold onto it. You've sure as shit got my interest. You *are* fascinating. And intelligent. Funny. Kind. Amazing."

I'm six seconds away from climbing onto Liam's lap and gluing my lips to his, when car tires grind on the gravel drive. I turn and spy a strange vehicle coming up from the road.

"Dinner's here," Liam says, sitting forward. "Hold that thought while I pay the driver and get our food. Meet me in the kitchen."

I watch Liam walk off toward the waiting vehicle. He's still tall, beautiful, and essentially graceful, even with a slight limp leftover from his college football injury. We've been together, uninterrupted for several days, and still being near him makes the butterflies come alive in my core. I'm still so diverted by his beauty that it's difficult to concentrate.

A few minutes later, when we're in the kitchen and he's busy organizing our plates, I watch him work. I have trouble believing it's really him, that he's really here, and that we're really together.

"Penny for your thoughts?" Liam asks, casually sliding a plate in front of me. It's loaded with good things, like filet mignon stuffed with bacon, cheese, herbs, and grilled to perfection. Beside that, there's a baked sweet potato loaded with gobs of savory butter. Rounding out the exceptional meal is a pile of asparagus drenched in creamy lemon butter sauce.

The meal, as spectacular as it is, doesn't distract me. Every neuron in my mind fires on the idea of Liam Gold in my kitchen, wrangling dinner. This image is downright domestic. I like it, almost too much.

"He can cook, too." I smile. Of course he can.

He cocks an eyebrow at me, taking his own plate, sitting at the table across from me.

"Is that really what you were thinking?" he asks, lifting a forkful of sweet potato to his mouth. "You looked like you had something else going on."

I shake my head. "Just distracted by you in my kitchen," I freely admit. "I could get used to it."

Liam half smiles. "In that case, yes, I can cook. I'm no gourmet chef like some of your friends in town, but I can hold my own."

"One night soon, cook for me," I say. "Let me watch you."

There's a vague hint of color rising in his cheeks, but he just nods and smiles.

Our meals are excellent, but it's dessert that will always stick with me. Liam ordered two slices of cheesecake, but that's not all. There's a jar of caramel syrup and a can of spray whipped cream to go with them.

"I was thinking we could take our time with dessert," Liam offers, a wicked gleam in his eye. "I was thinking I'd like to eat mine off your belly – *and other places*."

Jesus. My cock twitches, stiffening with just the mention of something creative like that. I imagine the places I could apply some whipped topping – then lick it off – and the image in my head makes me dizzy.

I've been making all the first moves, but this time I'm the one getting moved on. Liam reaches up to my shirt, deftly opening the first button with one hand, then then next and the next. In just a few seconds he's got my shirt completely open, my chest exposed. He yanks at the tails, untucking them from my jeans.

"Lie back," he insists, pushing me backward against the edge of the stout kitchen table that came with the house. The realtor told me the table was two hundred years old and made from a single slab of hand-hewn heart pine trunk. In other words, it's sturdy.

Liam reaches down, circling his big hands under my thighs. The next thing I know, in one swift move, he lifts me up onto the table top, then not so gently shoves me down so I am laying flat, looking up at the ceiling. That's when he climbs on top, straddling me on his knees with a can of whipped cream in one hand and a jar of caramel in the other.

"This is gonna be fun," he states, eyes flashing devilishly.

He tips the jar of caramel syrup over my exposed chest, a sly grin wrapping his perfect face. The stuff drizzles onto my skin in lacy patterns and globs that begin to soften and drip down.

"Oops! Let me get that for you!" Liam cries, almost laughing.

He descends upon me, tongue first, lapping up the thick, sweet spillage. He licks me in long, sexy strokes, circling my nipples, tweaking my buds with his teeth. He sucks and slurps, cleaning all the syrup off my body before coming up for air.

"Would you like some cream with that?" he asks, pleased with himself.

He squirts the whipped cream all over me, painting a design on my belly, pausing only long enough to undo my belt and the button and zipper on my slacks. I laugh and groan in equal measure.

"Just can't stop myself." He yanks my pants and shorts down, exposing my stiff cock to his teasing attentions.

He sprays whipped cream along the length of my shaft, then trails back up to my belly before diving in to lap up the sweetness like a happy cat. He starts at my ribcage, working his way down, careful not to smear his handiwork before licking it up with an enthusiastic tongue.

The last bit he gets to is the heavy dose of whipped topping painted down my cock.

"Mmmm…" he hums. "Look at this."

Liam takes his time, teasing, nipping, licking, slurping slowly, before taking me fully into his mouth. When he finally does, I'm already so hard, so tense, so past ready to explode into his throat I can barely contain myself. I sit up, gripping the sides of his head with steadying hands, showing him the best angle, slowing his speed, urging him on.

He swallows me deep, his enthusiasm boundless.

"That's it," I growl, trying to hold out. "Oh, fuck. You feel good on me."

He moans, his tongue ridging the head of my cock, sending me straight over the edge. I feel the wellhead swell, then lift. A second later, I lose it. The dam holding back the flood breaks. Liam takes it all - swallowing, lapping up every drop, his tongue never relaxing until I force him back. Then I pull him up on top of me inside my arms.

"Damn, you're good at that," I huff, my breath short.

He laughs. He just laughs. Then he presses his lips to mine, letting me taste myself on him. It's a salty, sweet, creamy mix of sex and dessert. It's perfect.

"Don't ever stop being you," I whisper. I want him like this, laughing against me, making me blow to pieces inside his embrace, forever. I don't care what it takes to keep him. I'm going to give it everything I have.

"Sure thing, sweet stuff," he says.

We're both sticky and sweet and more then ready for a shower.

CHAPTER TWELVE

LIAM

I put down my black metal American Express card, sliding it across the counter to the cashier after she gives me the total for my purchase. She takes the card, hands it back to me, and points to the machine to my right.

"Insert the chip inside the slot, please," she instructs, her words delivered in a monotone. She all but rolls her eyes at me.

I've never had my own credit card before. The closest I've ever come is the meal plan card at Virginia Tech, but that didn't have an RFID chip. The cashier always had to swipe it herself. That seems so long ago. I can't seem to get used to this new technology, but I'm starting to get used to the bottomless credit limit. Grayson gave it to me and said, "Consider it a perk of being my boyfriend."

"Sorry," I say to the cashier, slipping the chip into the machine while she bags my hot air gun and long handled scraper.

She nods, chewing her cud, cutting her eyes at me. "You're that guy's boyfriend, right?" she asks. "The crazy rich guy from California?"

She smirks like she knows all my secrets.

"I remember you," she says. "You used to collect cans and plastic bottles at the drive-in after the late show. I remember seeing you and that crazy looking dog of yours out there with a trash bag and a long stick with a nail on the end."

I can't help it. My face flushes red. There was a time when people asked, 'Didn't you used to be that football player?' Now all I am is 'that guy's boyfriend.'

I hear her laughing, whispering to her co-worker as I turn away, heading out the door to my truck. Together, they cackle behind my back. In the parking lot I catch an errant, curious glance from a woman and a young man who looks like he's her son. I instantly suspect they, too, recognize me as 'that guy's boyfriend.' Grayson is the talk of the town since he's back in Virginia—and that makes me the prime target for everyone's gossip.

I don't know these people and I don't know why I care, but my insecurities get the best of me sometimes.

Grayson flew to Boston a couple days ago to meet with the people he's trying to sell his company to. Since he left, except for sleeping all by myself for the first time in many weeks, I've been working pretty much nonstop on the renovation. I'm only three weeks into the job and the transformation is already amazing. We're bringing the majestic dignity of this old gilded-age house back from the brink. I pulled out some dropped-ceiling tiles in one of the upstairs bedrooms yesterday and was astonished to find perfectly preserved plaster ceilings with intricately sculpted handmade medallions and cornice moldings. Why anyone would ever cover up that kind of craftsmanship is beyond me, but I was happy to see it. I expect the rest of the rooms will reveal similar finely detailed hand work. I just wish Grayson was here to see it with me. The roofing contractors and tile guys working on the bathrooms weren't nearly as excited as I was.

Tonight, I'm working on my own place.

The 'Caretaker's Cottage,' as Grayson calls it, is more than adequate for my needs, but whoever did the renovation on it cut some serious corners that need to be fixed. The kitchen has gleaming, black granite countertops and custom-built cabinets, but the floors are covered in cheap, faux wood done in vinyl. It's one step above cheap linoleum, and it's got to go.

I'm laying down terra cotta tile in the kitchen and baths, but first I've got to peel up this plastic stuff. It promises to be a long, sweaty night working with the hot-air blow gun and the scraper. I've got to melt the glue and then peel the layers of vinyl up from the sub-flooring.

I'm at it for hours, winding up shirtless, sweating, swearing, with a pile of torn, peeled flooring stacked in the corner by the refrigerator. The exposed sub-flooring is beneath my feet, mottled with residual glue. A zillion little bits of shredded plastic and adhesive dust my skin. My hair is grainy with the shit, and the blow gun makes the whole place smell like an industrial incinerator. It's going to take weeks to get the chemical smell out of the house. But it'll be worth it.

"What in the hell are you doing?"

I start, looking up from my work. Grayson stands in the threshold between the hallway and the kitchen. He's wearing a fancy suit, his hands thrust in his pockets, a puzzled expression on his face. I've missed him so much it hurts. I did not expect that feeling.

He looks at me, meeting my eyes, bemused inquiry filling his expression.

I'm so glad he's home. I missed him more than I had a right to.

Beau missed him too. Instead of raising hell and barking at our unexpected intruder, Beau runs to Grayson, wagging

his tail, looking up at him hoping for some acknowl-
edgement.

Grayson reaches down, scratching Beau between his ears
with a grin and genuine affection.

"Hey buddy," he says. "Nice to see you too. I'm glad
I'm home."

I don't bother to answer Grayson's question about what
I'm doing. I don't even care what his question was. I drop my
long-handled scraper, letting it hit the floor with a dramatic
'thwack!' The hot blow gun can lie there unused for the rest
of the week for all I care. Grayson is home and I plan to let
him know he was missed.

"God, you're a sight for sore, lonely eyes," I huff, wrapping
my arms around him, nuzzling his neck. He smells good - of
aftershave and clean gabardine wool with just a hint of
commercial air travel (but first class). "I missed you so much."

I never missed anyone like this before, not since we graduated and went off to separate colleges. That's what this felt
like—except six times worse.

I hold Grayson tight, not wanting to let go. I didn't like
being here all alone. I've been back in Abingdon for years,
but suddenly the town felt alien without Grayson to move
through it with me.

"I missed you too," he whispers into my neck. "I missed
you something awful. I wanted you in Boston. I wanted you
there to enjoy it with me. It was no fun on my own."

He steps back, looking around at the mess I've made.
"Now tell me what the heck you're doing?"

I explain it to him, showing him the tile I'm planning to
lay down when I have scraped all this nasty plastic shit up.

"This cottage, just like the main house, is part of the same
historic property," I say, trying to justify my effort and the
expense. "It deserves quality. I'm paying for this myself. I

figure if I'm going to live here, I'm going to take some ownership of it."

Grayson accepts my response, but argues with me about who is paying for it. In truth, he's paying for all of it since he's paying my salary. We can quibble over the details later.

"We'll work it out," he says, squeezing my hand. "This isn't what I need to talk to you about. Do you have anything to drink in this place? I really could use a beer or a glass of something peaty."

All I have is beer, so that's all I can offer. I open a cold bottle straight from the fridge, handing it to Grayson, painfully aware of how grubby I look all covered with powdered plastic and glue.

"Let me go get a shower," I say. "I'm a sweaty, sticky, hot mess."

Grayson shakes his head. "In a few minutes," he insists. "Come sit with me just a little while. It's important."

I hate it when he gets all serious and urgent like this. I'm always afraid of the worst. I don't even know what the worst could be, but that doesn't stop me from dreading it.

With our beers in hand, we migrate into the living room. Grayson drops onto the big, overstuffed couch looking exhausted and distracted. I park myself in a comfortable club chair across from him, sitting forward, forearms resting on my knees, my posture attentive.

"It looks like the deal is going through," he says. "They're finishing up the last of their due diligence. The next step is to put the details in front of the SEC for a review. Once it's in their hands, it's going to get out to the media that I'm selling, and all hell is going to break loose."

I nod, not really understanding how—if at all—any of this impacts me.

"I don't want any part of the media circus that's about to start up," he says. "And I don't want to talk to any of the board members until it's done, either. I've discussed it with Justin at Nicolai. He suggested I get out of the country for a few weeks and go somewhere where the media has difficulty reaching."

A few weeks?! My heart sinks to my feet. The idea of doing without him for so long… it breaks my heart.

"Jeez, Gray, I don't know—I don't want you away for that long—"

"I'm really hoping you'll go with me," Grayson interjects, the sound of doubt weighing in his tone. "I know it's a lot to ask -to expect you to just drop everything and fly off with me. It's shitty of me to even hope for it, but I am."

Go with him? Is he serious?

The worried expression on his face tells me he's extremely serious. Doubt spikes lines into the corners of his eyes. His usually full, sweet lips flatten. He's expecting me to say 'no' and that's got him worried.

"Can Beau come?" I ask, already certain of the answer.

Grayson's flat expression of concern quickly morphs, turning up into a satisfied smile. He relaxes where he sits.

"Of course," he says. "There's no way we'd leave him."

"Where are we going?" I ask, feeling excitement at the idea of traveling already building. I've traveled all over the country playing football, but my sightseeing was usually restricted to the insides of hotel rooms and stadiums. I went to London once for an exhibition game, and to Beijing for the Olympics, but that was like living inside a luxury prison camp. I've never actually taken a vacation.

"Anguilla," Grayson replies, giving me a sheepish grin, squeezing my fingers. "An island in the Caribbean. I own a house there. It's nice and exceedingly private. We can leave as soon as you want to"

It'll take a couple days to shut down the renovation project. The tile crew is right in the middle of tiling two bathrooms, and that can't be halted mid-project. Other than that, I think I can pay everyone else off and have them keep their schedules open in a month or so.

It'll be good to get out of this town and away from all the knowing looks and murmured innuendos. It'll be good to go somewhere new where no one knows me, where I'm not viewed as an opportunist – *a gold digger*. It'll be great to just be able to be with Grayson out in public and not worry what anyone else thinks.

"And we're taking my private jet," Grayson adds, his sheepish smile turning puckish, eyebrows arching wickedly. "Doesn't that sound fun?"

It really does.

If I wasn't a stinky, sticky, filthy mess, I'd pull him onto my lap and let him know precisely how impressed I am. Instead, I decide to show him.

"I need a shower," I tell him, keeping my tone dry for effect. "I'd like some company. Would you care to volunteer? Or do I have to do it all alone?"

Grayson blinks, then beams while reaching up, tugging at his tie, loosening it.

"I'm in," he says, standing, pulling me with him. Despite my sweat and dusty filth, he pulls me close. He comes up on his toes to kiss me tenderly, lips pressing to mine, teeth gently nicking my lips and tongue. The intimacy of his kiss makes my knees tremble. My cock stiffens to attention almost instantly. Grayson feels that shift and he responds with fingers firmly stroking me. "Mmm," he whispers, his tongue tracing my jawline, his breath warming my skin. "I don't want you ever using this all alone anymore. I want you to share—always share—with me. Only me."

"Only you," I repeat, happy for the chance to say it. I return his kisses, wrapping him up in a big bear hug. "You've ruined me for anyone else. Thank you."

CHAPTER THIRTEEN

GRAYSON

*T*here are so many damn people who think I shouldn't be messing around with a man who used to live in his truck. From Tony's bold judgments against Liam to the smirking, sideways glances I catch out of the corner of my eye, I see it everywhere I go. Everyone has petty, jealous assumptions about us. It makes me rage—but it makes me even angrier for Liam.

I have zero doubt that at some point in the future, Liam won't give a shit what these insignificant people think. But right now, he's still trying to find his way out of his old life and into this new one; a life I hope he'll share with me for a long time to come.

It feels like he and I—as a couple—came together fast, but it was more than a decade in the making. I started falling in love with Liam Gold when I was fourteen years old. I never stopped falling. I'm still in free fall, and this trip makes me feel for him even more deeply. That's why it kills me that anyone would think ill of him, much less have the nerve to air their unwanted, unqualified opinions in public.

I may not be able to control how the assholes in

Abingdon behave, but I can wield a lot more control out in the rest of the world.

"Jesus, is that yours?" Liam asks, leaning on the door, his nose pressed against the car window, peering out at the tarmac and the jet parked there.

"It is," I admit, leaning over, resting my hand on his thigh, doing my best to see the world through Liam Gold's very sweet, wonder-filled eyes. It's hard for anyone to understand what a billion dollars looks like. I *still* don't get it myself most of the time. Seeing Liam's reactions make me even more aware of how grateful I am. The jet is painted silver and black without any logos or recognizable marks except what the FAA demands. When you're a billionaire, you no longer need to advertise your brand.

Liam turns to Beau, eyebrows raised. "Dude, we're going up in that," he says. "You up for it?"

All Beau can do is wag. He has no clue what's coming.

The sleek little jet looks like it's doing Mach-10 while sitting perfectly still on the blacktop. I guess it's impressive to someone who's never seen a Bombardier Challenger 650 up close and personal. It's still impressive to me every time I climb aboard it, but then I know precisely how fast, efficient, and unapologetically over-the-top luxurious it is. That's why I bought it.

"That's ridiculous," Liam observes, grinning like a kid, wonder overflowing in his expression. "And wicked cool!"

We don't have many bags, as the plan I sold to Liam was that we'd shop for suitable warm weather clothing once we got to the island. Anguilla is a tiny place, but it's got no shortage of tourist destinations and high-end shopping among the long list of diversions. It's like Beverly Hills without the California sales tax.

We board the aircraft, climbing the stairs up to the cabin of the small, private jet, with just our carry-ons in hand and

Beau on a leash tethered snugly to Liam's hand. I've made a point of ensuring everyone we're likely to encounter on this little excursion knows Liam is a lifelong friend, not just my boyfriend.

"Mr. Ellis, so good to see you again," Captain Paul Hartley, the pilot and commander of the flight crew says to me as I cross the threshold. He stands to the left of the main cabin door where we board, just outside the cockpit, eager to shake my hand. Marilyn Cooper, the Chief Flight Attendant, stands beside him, looking a little nervous. She welcomes me too, then gives me the chance to introduce Liam and Beau—who steals the show—making a great impression on everyone.

Judging by Liam's startled expression, he didn't expect a welcoming committee. When Marilyn reaches to take his carry-on, he pulls it closer under his arm in a defensive manner. Marilyn smiles sweetly.

"It'll be right at your feet," she says, motioning toward the storage bins beside the comfortable seats in the main cabin area. "I promise. I'm just stowing it for you."

Liam relinquishes his bag reluctantly while looking around in awe. The interior of the state of the art jet is sleek, with clean lines, using only the prettiest real wood, brushed metal, and top-quality leather finishes to give the thing the feel of a luxurious ocean-going cruise liner. Everything inside is built for comfort and convenience - from the armrest mounted media console to the plush leather seats, softly padded carpeting, and thoughtful interior design. There are cup holders at the tops of every armrest, and more along the side rail shelves under the oversized cabin windows. While it's too early in our travels to enjoy the benefit of it yet, I know the craft was designed and constructed with quiet travel in mind. The big engines may roar outside during the flight, but inside it's as quiet as floating on a cloud.

"Mr. Ellis, what would you like to drink?" another flight attendant asks as Marilyn rolls out a snack tray loaded with veggies, dips, crackers, cheese, and other savories.

"Just a soda water," I say. "In a little while I may want something more."

She nods, then turns her attention to Liam. "And you, Mr. Gold?" she asks, smiling at him. "We have a fully stocked bar, as well as soft drinks, Pellegrino, Perrier…"

"I'll take a Coke," Liam says, not waiting for her to finish the lengthy list. "Just a Coke."

"Sure thing, Mr. Gold," she quips. "Right away."

Liam doesn't know what to make of any of this. He's thoroughly freaked out, but he's trying hard to play it cool.

"Here, sit across from me," I say, directing us toward a pair of seats facing one another along the aft side of the cabin, right where Marilyn stuffed our carry-ons.

Liam settles himself down into the oversized chair with its soft, leather-clad cushions. Beau curls up in a perfect circle at his master's feet, his head resting on his hind legs and tail, eyes up and attentive.

Liam reaches down to stroke Beau several times, calling him 'Good,' then he peers across the wide gulf between us with concern darkening his eyes. "I should have asked for something more potent," he tells me. "I wasn't thinking. I was just so distracted by…"

His wandering eyes fall still upon the screen in front of him.

"…everything," he half mumbles, his eyes narrowing, focusing on the small screen. 'How is there live television on an airplane?" he asks, pointing toward the monitor. "It's CNN. How is that possible?"

I shake my head, shrugging. "Satellites and service providers?" I offer. "The jet has its own IP address. There's not much you can't get. Television is the least of it, at least in good weather."

Liam hauls in a deep breath, then exhales just as deeply. He lets go of a good deal of tension, allowing his body to relax, melting into the plush seats. A second later the flight attendant appears with our beverages, laying small cocktail napkins down below them. Liam lifts his Coke, guzzling most of it in one motion. Our flight attendant – surprised by his tremendous thirst—drops what she's doing to fetch him another one.

"Here you go," she says, her cheeks flushed red, eyelashes batting deliberately. "If you need another, don't hesitate, even for a second, to ask. Now, gentlemen, fasten your seatbelts. We'll be departing soon."

It's clear my talk with the flight crew about treating Liam with deference and respect sunk in. That said, I think this girl likes Liam almost as much as I do—and in exactly the same way. I can't muster up jealousy against her, as I know there's no need whatsoever. I can't help but be entertained by her flirting. It's sexy watching someone try to gain *my lover's* attention, while he remains completely oblivious.

"I could get used to this," Liam announces as soon as she's gone. He stretches out his long legs, his boot-clad feet hooking around mine teasingly. He's got a glass of Coke in one hand and a small plate filled with healthy snacks perched on the ledge beneath the window by his other hand. His smiling eyes fix on mine.

"Which part?" I ask as the pilot revs up the engines, releasing the breaks, backing us gently away from the gate. "The girl flirting with you, or me getting off on watching it?"

By his instant, shocked expression, I realize I've caught him off guard. He's surprised by my question. Liam Gold *almost* blushes.

"You're crazy," he responds, lowering his voice. "She wasn't doing that."

I doubt she was doing it intentionally. Maybe she was just being overly friendly. *Still...*

"I don't mind," I say, brushing off my comments. "What is it you could get used to? All of it, I hope."

He nods, smirking shyly. "All of it," he admits. "Like I belong here. Like some insufferable, rich asshole who flies around in a Leer jet like he owns the whole world."

Like me?

"It's a Bombardier Challenger 650," I say, realizing I sound precisely like an insufferable ass. "Leer Jets are tiny and not nearly as comfortable as this one."

Liam laughs, wagging his finger at me. "Just like that!" he says, telling me what I already know. "You'll have me drinking expensive Scotch and eating caviar before all this is said and done."

Just then the plane turns, heading down the runway, picking up speed at a breathtaking pace. I'm shoved backwards into my seat by the unexpected G-force, while Liam is propelled forward straight into me. He catches himself with hands gripping at my armrests. We're face to face; he's almost in my lap. The plane lifts off, tipping up sharply into the sky. Both of us catch our breath, staring into one another's eyes.

If I could have planned that, I would have. He still has the grace and acrobatic reflexes of a cat. That Coke he was holding is still in his hand, not a drop spilled.

"I hope this is never said and done," I say to him, breathing the heated words onto his lips. "I'll feed you caviar with a monogrammed silver spoon. I'll buy a Scotch distillery and put your name on it, if that's what it takes to keep you."

Liam blinks, then bites his lip, which just kills me. *I want to kiss that lip.*

I lift my hand, circling it around his neck, pulling him down to me. Our lips meet, teeth and tongues clashing, then finding a hungry rhythm. The next thing I know, Liam is on my lap and I've forgotten momentarily where we are when I feel the jet level off. The pilot comes on over the intercom, speaking the following:

"Good morning everyone, this is Captain Hartley. We'll reach cruising altitude shortly, maintaining airspeed at about eight hundred fifty kilometers per hour with a nice tailwind. I expect we'll reach the airport at Anguilla in just under three hours. The weather looks clear all the way out over the Atlantic, so relax and enjoy the flight."

Liam sits back, keeping my shoulders in his firm grip. He grins down at me, licking his lips, his pale eyes flashing.

"I can't wait to get you naked on the beach," he tells me. "The things I want to do…"

"Yeah?" I ask, pleased he's thinking creatively.

I can think of a few things to do too.

* * *

WHEN YOU'RE out over the Atlantic, cutting a swath above the Doldrums, flying dead center between Bermuda and the Bahamas, the ocean looks like it is the beginning and the end of the world. There is no land visible from our porthole windows midway through the flight, but once we're on approach to our destination, the view is altogether captivating.

Anguilla appears out on the rim of the world like a tiny green fingerling floating in a sea of aquamarine. The nearer we get, the more of the island landscape takes shape. Our descent shows us an island with roads, towns, and dense population. Still, more natural beauty clings to its steeply sloped volcanic hills and pristine, white sand beaches than perhaps any place remaining in the first world. The colors here are unlike any existing in continental North America. The blue of the ocean is so intensely blue-green as to look almost cartoonish. The ochre red of the cliffs reminds you of rusting metal gleaming red hot in the sun. The sand is the shade of bleached bone.

"God, that's gorgeous," Liam whispers, his forehead stuck to the glass, his gaze peering steadily down.

The pilot tips the plane, preparing us for approach. Our air speed slows dramatically.

"Just wait," I tease. "The house here is amazing."

Liam looks over at me, tearing his eyes away from the stunning view. "Better than Abingdon?"

I want to tell him that the house in Abingdon is great and all, but the only reason I bought it was for sentimental reasons all having to do with him. The house at Anguilla – like all my others – is reflective of me and my tastes, my expectations, and my net worth. (Real estate is a wonderful tax shelter.)

Instead of telling him all that, I just nod, offering a meek smile. "Yes," I say. "Better than Abingdon."

So much better, in fact, that I had to have Mrs. Hill, my housekeeper from Mountain View, come out ahead of us with staff to open the house and get it ready for our arrival. There were linens to be freshened, rooms to be cleaned, groceries to be bought, pumps to be primed, pools to be filled, and who knows what all else to do. All I know is that Mrs. Hill has been in Anguilla a week and as late as yesterday afternoon, she was still stressing out about being ready in time.

"I don't want your friend thinking the people who look

out after you are incompetent," Hill told me over the phone. "He'll have you second guessing keeping me on."

As if that would ever happen.

I didn't warn Liam about the flight crew. I'd better alert him to Mrs. Hill and her gang of domestics. Otherwise, he may feel more than a little crowded.

"My housekeeper, Mrs. Hill, flew out last week to open the place," I offer casually.

Liam gives me a curious look.

"She's wonderful. You're going to love her. I couldn't do without her."

I really couldn't.

"Okay," he says, returning his attention out the window. The island below us gets closer and closer, the fields of mottled green now breaking up, rendering individual trees, shrubs, and crops below us. "I guess that makes sense, that you have *staff*. I guess you kind of have to."

I guess I do.

Liam lifts his gaze, returning his attention to me.

"Does she know about... *me?*"

This strikes me as an odd question.

"Yeah," I say. "Of course, she does. She knows about *us*. Why?"

He shakes his head, shrugging. "I dunno," he admits. "It's just odd for me. I'm not used to any of this. Not the money. Not the pampering. Not the people who are all part of it. I'm not used to any of it. I don't know how to behave around people who work for you. It's awkward. I don't know where I fit."

I reach across the space between us, leaning deep, so I can take Liam's hand in mine. I circle my fingers around his palm, snugging it firmly in my grip.

"Try not to overthink it," I advise. "Just let it be what it is and enjoy it when you can. You fit right beside me, with me.

We're a couple. My staff all know that. They have no uncertainty where you fit, so you shouldn't either."

I know it's not that easy, but I'm hoping that with time and encouragement, he'll find that his place in this is just as I've said: right beside me.

A moment later the jet's altitude drops and the engines reverse, slowing our progress. The nose tips up as the land beneath us rises fast. A second later the wheels touch down on black-topped tarmac. The tires scream from friction with the runway. A rapid descent followed by a swift taxi to the tiny island airport, we halt a few moments later by a small white building with a Range Rover parked in front of it.

I peek out my port window and see Hill climb out of he SUV. She looks tanned and relaxed, dressed all in pastel pinks and whites, her blond hair whipping in the wind. She lifts her hand, flattening it over her eyes to shield them from the intense Caribbean sunshine. Her expression is all happy, full of curiosity.

I've missed all of this, so much. *This is going to be a fun little vacation with Liam.* Now he gets to see how I really live.

CHAPTER FOURTEEN

LIAM

"Grayson, you didn't tell me how stunning this man is," Mrs. Hill says, flipping her long blond hair back. She tips her Gucci shades up on top of her head and takes my free hand between both of hers. She holds my hand tight, just gazing at me—*a little too long*—making me squirm.

"He's is," Grayson says, shouldering his bag. He reaches into her grip, freeing me from her clutches. He takes my hand inside his, possessively. "And he's all mine," he says to her. He then turns his addresses to me. "Liam, this is Hill. She's something of a tiger mom, so don't take any shit from her."

Hill grins slyly, winking at me. "That's the nicest thing he's said about me all week," she observes. "For what it's worth, it takes a tiger mom to keep this one in line."

Hill nods toward the sparkling black SUV parked a few paces away, lifting the keys. "Lunch is ready," she says. "Hope you two are hungry. And per your request, Gray, I organized a shopping venture for this afternoon."

Grayson nods. "Perfect. Thank you."

We set off with Mrs. Hill at the wheel. I'm just taking it all in, sitting in the back, watching the odd, quirky little island houses and low cinder block buildings pass by my window. The landscape is windswept, tropical, and colonial, with every man-made surface painted brightly in deep colorful hues and pastels. Yellow and pink dominate, but there are orange and blue houses, a green hotel, and a two-story auto parts store that's lavender and teal. The streets are barely paved in the little town we pass through as we leave the vicinity of the airport. Most of the side streets aren't paved at all.

Something about the place seems incongruous. The few people we see on the streets are either very old or very young, casually dressed, wearing sandals or barefoot, and their skin naturally dark or deeply tanned from the Caribbean sun overhead. This place doesn't look like a billionaire's hideaway. It looks like a leeward landscape that time forgot.

"Have you ever been to the West Indies?" Mrs. Hill asks, peering at me in her rear-view mirror.

I shake my head. *'I haven't been anywhere in a long, long time,'* I think to myself. To her, I respond. "No, ma'am."

She smiles at me. "You don't need to call me 'ma'am,'" she says. "But I appreciate the good manners. You're going to enjoy Anguilla. Liam's house here is magnificent. The beaches are the most beautiful in the world, the food is outstanding, and there's something different to do every single night."

Looking around at the tiny village we're just leaving behind us, it's difficult to imagine much in the way of entertainment or nightlife - maybe a steel drum band playing a local dive bar. Then, up ahead of us, I get my first glimpse of the Anguilla from the tourist brochures. It's a collection of villas perched on a hill behind a high wall and a heavy metal gate, contemporary in design and construction (as opposed to the colonial style of the buildings in the village). These buildings are constructed in concrete, steel, and glass, built like a fortress against some unseen nemesis. There's a tasteful metal and stone sign at the gate, done in elegant raised lettering that reads, "SeaBleu Villas Resort".

As we drive by the gate, I glimpse manicured landscaping and a man in khaki shorts with a wide-brimmed straw hat driving a golf cart. There's a bag of expensive looking clubs piled in the back.

Anguilla is obviously an 'us and them' sort of place. The locals live inland, away from the beautiful beaches. The tourists with their fistfuls of dollars cling to the coastline.

Mrs. Hill navigates us onto a seaside byway with the impossibly blue Caribbean ocean on our left and the rising, tropical landscape on our right. The brightly painted wooden houses and watering holes give way to stucco clad hotels and mansions, terra cotta tile roofs, and sprawling golf courses.

"There's my place," Grayson says, peering up the lane we've just turned onto. He glances back at me, looking for some kind of reaction.

The house is huge--at least the part of it I can glimpse behind a high concrete wall and towering canopy of flowering trees that give the neighborhood the feel of a tropical rainforest.

Mrs. Hill taps a button on a remote attached to the SUV's sun visor. Ahead of us, an imposing iron gate slowly slides open as we approach, then quickly glides closed as we pass through into another world.

The wall and carefully placed shrubbery at the gate conceal a large, rolling lot landscaped to manicured perfection with flowering plants and fruit-bearing trees. The lawn is planted with a dense, soft grass and bordered with romantic, cobblestone walkways. A hundred yards away a lawn crew works on ladders, pruning a tree heavily laden with fruit. They're obviously local people. They're small in stature, chestnut toned skin, dressed in worn, stained work pants, all wearing lime green long-sleeve t-shirts bearing the logo of a landscaping company. One of them turns his head as we pass, his big brown eyes peering at the darkened glass of our SUV. He watches us as we move up the cobbled drive, only dropping his gaze when we glide around the far side of the house.

'Us and them.'

What comes next feels a little like something out of a scene from *Downton Abbey* or *The Queen*.

Ten people are lined up on the flagstone drive next to what appears to be a side entrance to the big house. They're standing attentively, some in uniform, others in street clothes, all of them clearly in the employ of Grayson. *His household staff.* It starts to finally dawn on me what it means that Grayson Ellis is a billionaire. Not only does he have everything a person could possibly want, he also has people at his beck and call.

I can't even imagine how complicated that must make his life. And it makes sense that so many people are invested in who he's dating.

The people around Gray simper and smile, offering deferential handshakes to their master as we move through the reception line. With me, most of them just nod and smile warmly. I try to make eye contact. I try to remember their names. It goes so fast it's almost impossible.

A pretty young woman named Amelia takes my bag from my shoulder, refusing to take no for an answer.

"To your room," she says, speaking in an accent that's familiar but also exotic and melodic. She grins at me, shaking her head. "Relax, Mr. Gold," she says, goading. "You're safe with us here."

I feel she may be telling me the truth.

She takes Grayson's bag too, leaving us with Mrs. Hill and a couple other members of the staff.

"We've prepared a light lunch for you," a not quite middle-aged man dressed in billowing, indigo blue cotton pants and a pristine white t-shirt says. He's got fierce, hazel colored eyes and a shaved head. If it were not for the small, slumping hat on his head advertising his profession as chef, I'd peg him for a personal trainer. "Grilled Local Crayfish with sweet plantains, grilled vegetables with mango, traditional rice and peas, served with ginger vinaigrette."

Oh, good God, that sounds absolutely astounding.

"It's ready to be served on the main veranda, whenever you're ready."

Grayson smiles, nodding. "Just give us a few minutes to freshen up and we'll be right there."

We haven't even made it all the way in the door, and I can already taste salt air blowing in from the ocean.

"I'll meet you two upstairs in ten," Mrs. Hill says. "I took the liberty of bringing some things from home, guessing you wouldn't pack anything sensible for the tropics. Everything is unpacked and in the closet."

Grayson leans down, kissing Mrs. Hill on the cheek. "Thank you for taking such good care of us," he says. "The house looks great."

The house does look great--what little I've seen so far. There's a huge vase filled with fresh, tropical flowers in the foyer ahead of us. The plaster walls are adorned with original artworks, each one illuminated from a small spotlight recessed in the ceiling above. As we make our way toward the main gallery, it's clear that every open space is adorned with flowers, their sweet scent filling the fresh, sea swept air. The cobblestone floors are covered with woven grass and Persian rugs. There's an unselfconscious chic to this space that whispers of old money mingled with new. It's not a bad combination.

"Come on up to the main floor," Grayson urges, pulling my attention away from the lengthy expanse of corridors going off in each direction of the compass. "This is the service level. We won't spend a lot of time down here."

The service level? Jesus, the basement of this place looks like a fine estate. I steel myself, not sure what to expect topside.

I'm not disappointed.

We emerge at the top of the stairs into a large, open air gallery overlooking the most spectacular ocean view I've even beheld. Grayson's house is situated on a high cliff a hundred yards above the rock and sand beach below. We're high enough up to catch a cool ocean breeze without the salt-laden humidity that comes with being at sea level. This space is indoors, but wide open to the natural space beyond. In fact, it's difficult to discern where indoors stops and outdoors begins. There are so many graduating spaces from one to the other.

"Our rooms are upstairs," Grayson says, nodding up to the next level.

The grand stairwell is cut from beautiful blond limestone, as are the balustrades and, I suspect, all the flooring as well. The exterior walls of the structure appear to be at least a foot and a half thick. It also looks like most of the interior walls are pocket doors which can be opened to create a wide, open space.

Mounting the top gallery, overlooking the main hall below and the lawn and roofline of the lower floors beyond that, I spy rooftop solar panels and an array positioned to the south of the house. There appears to be a cistern on each wing of the house, catching rainwater from the roof and sloping hills above the place.

It occurs to me, as I take in the construction details, that this house looks like it was built to withstand everything right up to a nuclear blast or a zombie apocalypse. It might be a good location to hide out following either one, that is, unless a hurricane comes – which is why (I suspect) this place is built as it is. The floating interior walls can be opened to allow the wind and water to move through without tearing the place to pieces. The low, flat rooflines without soffits or cantilevers give the wind nothing to grab onto. When the power goes out and the water pumping station on the island goes down, the solar system and cisterns can be deployed to run the household.

"Here we are," Grayson says, leading me into a wide corridor. "Our rooms."

Our 'rooms' are a house unto themselves. There are two bedrooms, a living room, a sitting room/office, a small kitchen, and dining area under a tidy canopy on a balcony outside. It overlooks the cliffs, beach, and a pool that's just yards away.

The closet where Mrs. Hill unpacked the items she brought for Grayson from California is larger than any bedroom I've ever had. It's not a closet so much as a fully equipped dressing room, complete with 360-degree mirrors.

"You seem a little stunned," Grayson observes, coming up to me as I stand in the middle of *'our bedroom'*, attempting to take it all in.

I guess I am.

"Just trying to wrap my head around it," I say. "It's a lot to… take in."

He steps closer, slipping his fingers into my hand. His expression is almost pained, and I feel guilty for causing that with my hesitation and inability to adequately accept all this as quickly as I ought to.

"It's just a house. Just things," he says. "Something for us to enjoy together."

I nod, trying hard to hide my concerns. "Okay," I say. "I know. It's just... a long way from where I come from."

A very long way. If anyone in my family had ever lived to see me standing in this room, they would have laughed and said, "You're dreaming!" Even after I got the scholarship to Tech, a distant cousin told me they'd made a mistake and they'd figure it out soon enough and send me, packing, back to Abingdon.

In the end, they were all right. I *was* delusional. I thought the dream come true would last, but it never does. I got hurt, and that was that. Virginia Tech and the NFL had no more need for me once my knees were blown up.

Looking back on all of it, I realize I was always just an actor playing a part – an imposter waiting to be found out. I always knew I didn't really belong under those stadium lights with all those thousands of people cheering my name at the top of their lungs. It was a delusion I let myself get swept up in.

I need to be careful to not get swept up in this dream.

"We should change clothes," Grayson says, squeezing my hand, giving me that disarming, sexy grin that melts me. "I bet I have some shorts here that'll fit you. You look good in my t-shirts, no matter what."

A half hour later we're lounging in shorts under a canvas shade not far from a fire pit where our crayfish and vegetables have been grilled to charbroiled perfection. The chef and his assistant lay out the spread for us, filling our tall crystal glasses with ice-cold sweet tea.

"Looks like you two have everything you need," Mrs. Hill says, checking in on us just as the chef plates up our exotic lunches. "The car will be downstairs at four o'clock to pick you up for shopping. I'll see you then."

Grayson nods, not replying. Instead he peers across the table at me. "You have everything you need?" he asks.

"I think so," I tell him, lifting my fork, preparing to dive in to this gourmet concoction of island deliciousness. "If not, I'm sure you'll see to it."

Grayson smirks. "You know I will."

* * *

THE TEN-MINUTE DRIVE to the southernmost tip of the island, to a small private community called Mead Cay, which is situated behind a tall, white stone masonry wall separating it from the rest of Anguilla, occurs without much fanfare. The one thing I take note of is the small number of neatly kept, modest houses along the beach road along our way. Those homes are few and far between, compared to the large number of hotels, resorts, and luxurious private homes lining the ocean front drive.

"How do regular people afford to live here?" I ask Grayson as I peer out at the view.

"They can't, really," he says. "The ones who do stay do something related to tourism to earn a living. They've probably inherited property. Otherwise, they can't usually stay. A lot of the young people go to St. Martin or the Bahamas. A lot go to the U.S."

It's the same story almost anywhere where there's natural beauty or valuable resources. The wealthy move in and push the locals away. It's the same in Abingdon and the mountains of Virginia, out west in places like Montana and Colorado, and even here, out on the edge of the world.

"Anguilla is a tax haven," Grayson states. "The thinking is that by attracting people like me who need to shelter a portion of their assets, they'll benefit from a trickle-down effect."

I peer up another dirt road, into a lane lined with faded pink shanties. A painfully thin dog strolls alone on the dirt path, but there's not a human soul to be seen.

Just then, we pass a small school house. It's a simple, cinder block building painted yellow, with tall windows and a wide, double front door. The main yard is dirt, with a broken down swing set in front and a rusty set of crumbling monkey bars. The kids have all gone home, but the school busses – three of them – have returned. They're parked in a dusty lot beside the school building, their faded paint jobs marred with rust and graffiti. Beside them, a nearby dumpster overflows with garbage, spilling out onto the ground.

"How's that trickle-down working out for them?" I ask, cutting my eyes at Grayson.

He shrugs. "Not sure," he admits. "Probably not so well."

While the local public schools have a lot to answer for, the exclusive shopping and entertainments offered at Mead Cay need not beg for any apologies. When I was in college and we played in Miami, I saw some places like this. Mead Cay is like South Beach without the bumper to bumper traffic.

It's quieter than Miami, but it retains all the glitz and high price tags, with a clientele who look more like Wall Street bankers and real estate moguls than self-made Silicon Valley billionaires. That said, the scenery is stunning. Mead Cay's nearly mile long shopping district is situated on a reinforced concrete battery overlooking a white sand beach. The sea beyond is crowded with massive yachts, small sailboats, a couple tall sailing ships, and countless small pleasure craft anchored in the bay.

"You'd look good in these," Grayson suggests, sliding a pair of sunglasses on my head, tucking them down on my nose.

He stands back to examine the image, then smiles, nodding. "Perfection!" he pronounces.

I glance in a nearby mirror to see what he sees.

The frames are white, oversized, with pitch black lenses. I look like some aged Hollywood producer.

"No," I say, removing the glasses, replacing them on the rack they came from.

Grayson grins at me. "Maybe not, but you do need sunglasses out here. Pick out a couple pairs you like."

A couple pairs? When the least expensive pair of shades is almost three hundred dollars, it's hard to justify one, much less two. But to Gray, this is *nothing*.

"One for out and about and one for the beach," Grayson says. "The beach pair is gonna get trashed."

Two pair of shades, a few pairs of shorts, a couple pairs of dressy slacks for going out, along with some shirts, and I don't even want to know what it all costs. I walk away when Grayson gives his card to the clerk.

"We're going to Versace next," he tells me. "Then maybe the Ferragamo store. We both need shoes."

Custom made Italian suits and loafers. *Why do I feel like I'm an imposter, living someone else's dream come true?*

"You will get used to this," Grayson assures me sometime later, as we're escaping an expensive boutique with our purchases. He's wisely discerned that I'm not altogether easy with all this conspicuous consumption. "We have the money. I can't give it away fast enough, so we have to spend some of it on ourselves. Just keep in mind, everything we buy was made by someone, sold by someone. The money we spend here pays people's bills. It's not all bad."

He's right – *sort of.* I wonder if I can ever get used to it, though.

Hours later, back at the house, with the sun setting behind the hills to the west of us, the sky to the east – out over the ocean – slowly transforms. The hue moves from pale blue to periwinkle, to a deep magenta, then to the most intense shade of cobalt blue popped with twinkling stars. Grayson and I lounge in the corner of a sun-warmed salt-water pool, drinking lemonade coolers.

It's beautiful here, magical really. The way the sky changes so quickly, an explosion of starlight firing overhead, where just moments ago the skies were streaked with orange-fired fingers of the setting sun is amazing. Out in the trees the birds quiet down, settling in for a long nap.

Earlier in the evening we had a supper of stone crab and conch with local vegetables, served to us in the open air on the rooftop patio overlooking a 360-degree view of the island. I learned over dinner that our chef is in Grayson's full-time employ. He, like Mrs. Hill, came from California to open the house, getting it ready for our visit. I learn that at least six others also traveled from the west coast to be here.

After dinner, and after we've moved to the pool, I ask Grayson, "How many people work for you?"

"I don't know exactly," he admits. "I know Hill has charge of the housekeeping staff and grounds. Chef has a staff. I have a PA, who's still in California handling things for me."

"A PA?" I ask, clueless.

"Personal assistant," he informs me. "Naomi. She's my go-to for all things work and social. She's like Mrs. Hill, but for everything outside the household."

Fascinating. I can't imagine having so many people so intimately familiar with every aspect of my life. He has so many he can't even number them all.

Grayson sits his empty glass on the edge of the pool, then reaches for me, hooking his thumbs under the waistband of my brand-new swim trunks. He tugs them down slightly, pulling me closer to him.

"We'll get you a PA," he teases. "Then your people and my

people can compare schedules and find some time for us to get together."

I shake my head, giving him a crooked smile. "I don't need a PA," I tell him. "I'll make time for you."

"Outstanding," he replies, pulling me so close our knees bump, then slide past each other. We're hip to hip, lip to lip, our breath warm in contrast to the rapidly cooling evening air. "Make time for me now?"

I bring my arms over his shoulders, draping them loosely, bringing us closer together.

"What did you have in mind?" I breath in his ear, wrapping my legs around his hips under the warm water, pressing my firming cock into his.

I've never had sex by the ocean, or in a swimming pool, or under the Milky Way, but I'm not opposed to the idea. This view, overlooking the phosphorescent sea with a dozen boats moored out in the water just off-shore, is spectacular. This kind of luxury is an aphrodisiac and, as much as I'm opposed to some aspects of it, I can't help but enjoy my good fortune.

Good food, wine coolers, and the tropical air all conspire to make both of us ready from almost the first brush of contact, but I want this to last. Instead of going right for the plunge, I take Grayson in my arms and turn him so his back is to me. Then I spread his arms out wide on the pool deck as I lay down a carpet of plush kisses over his shoulders, across his arms, down his back. He's got a beautiful form, and I haven't spent enough time paying tribute to it. I've been selfish and hurried. I've been over cautious and afraid. Tonight – *from now on* – I'm going to take my time and show Grayson just how much this all means – just how important he is to me.

"I'm sorry it's taken me awhile to figure all this out," I whisper against his ear, sliding my hand around his chest, pulling him against me. "The one thing I've never been confused about is you. I know how I feel about you, *about us.*"

Grayson leans back, relaxing against me, his head falling into the crook of my shoulder.

"Good," he says, his left hand falling to my thigh. "The rest of it will come together."

He turns inside my embrace, facing me. Once more we share a kiss, but this one isn't patient or chaste. It's hot, hungry, brimming with intention, and before I know it we're splashing in the water, wrestling. Then Grayson abruptly stops, backing away from me, rubbing the water from his eyes.

He glances out toward the ocean, then looks back at me.

"We should take this inside," he says. "Never know who's lurking out there with long lenses."

At first I think he's joking, or perhaps just being paranoid, but then it dawns on me – once more – that my beautiful, sweet, clever boyfriend is a billionaire. I've seen paparazzi shots of him in the tabloids. What he suggests wouldn't be so far beyond the realm of possibility.

"Okay," I say, reaching out a hand to him.

A few minutes later we're inside, tucked safely behind billowing curtains, still able to enjoy the warm ocean breezes, but beyond the reach of long lenses or prying eyes. We make love in a massive bed dressed in tight linen sheets scented with lemon blossoms. We drown in a sea of feather-light pillows, rolling in a tangle of arms and legs, asses and sweet lips.

Grayson cries out when I bring him to his peak, his body strung tight like an over tuned instrument. When he springs, it's with fists clutching sheets, his back arched, my hands gripping his hips while I drive in deep, finding my own secrets revealed in his depths.

"Oh fuck, baby," he preens, his voice breaking into the sheets. "Oh fuck, I love this with you. I love you."

I love you.

The breath catches in my chest. My brain freezes for a moment.

I love you.

Our bodies move like one thing. Our synchronous rhythm is perfect. He exhales and I breathe him in, then we reverse the process. He owns me. I possess him. We were made for this. We were made for one another, and we fit.

Moments later, lying still in one another's arms, Grayson's breathing deepens and evens out. His eyelids flutter. His lips part slightly. He drifts.

I watch him, marveling at just how beautiful he is, how sweet and boyish he looks, laying inside my arms like this. He loves me. What does that mean? I don't even know, but I know I want to try and find out.

He licks his lips, swallowing, then breathes in deeply.

"Tomorrow," he mumbles, sliding his hand around my bicep. "Tomorrow we're going to Mead Cay for dinner. A close friend of mine owns a place... I want him to meet you..."

Grayson drifts off again. I'm left to speculate, in the creeping darkness, about who this old friend is and what the odds are of anyone else in Grayson's circle living all the way out here on the edge of civilization. Clearly, there's more than just an acquaintance relationship. A tinge of jealousy pinches my psyche, but I try to push it away.

After all, he's asleep in *my* arms, purring like a contented kitten.

He loves me.
And I know I love him.

CHAPTER FIFTEEN

GRAYSON

I open my eyes reluctantly, not wanting to bring our perfect night to an end. Outside in the early morning sunrise, just beyond billowing curtains and open balcony doors and windows, the sound of waves crashing on the beach is about the most relaxing, sensuous sound a body can embrace. The only thing better is the rumble of Liam's gentle snores tickling my ear. He's snuggled around me, wrapping me up in a spoon embrace so comfortable and safe I don't want to move.

"Good morning, baby." His voice is filled with sleep, and his eyes are only half open. He presses his hot lips against the back of my neck, palms flat against my skin, squeezing my chest tight to his. He rocks his hips into my ass suggestively. I feel the wicked smile come to those lips when he does it.

The scent of fresh coffee and something salty wafts by, calling my attention.

"I think somebody made us breakfast," Liam purrs. "I heard someone come in, then leave, and now I smell coffee and eggs."

My stomach growls. I'm thirsty.

"Let's eat while it's hot," I suggest enthusiastically, rolling out of Liam's embrace even as he protests. He sits up, a scowl marring his gorgeous features. He stretches, yawning, then shakes off sleep.

Beau slept with us last night, making a big circle at the foot of the bed, snoring loudly. Now that Liam's awake, Beau stands, stretches, then leaps to the floor, wagging his tail.

"Pour me a cup of coffee?" Liam begs. "I've gotta take Beau out."

Mrs. Hill kept Beau while we were out shopping yesterday, but otherwise he's been with us. It's obvious he's not quite sure what to make of all this. He's cautious of the yard and of the pool. He's uncertain of the big bed we sleep in and he's curious about the things we do in it. Last night he watched us, unsure whether I was hurting Liam or he was hurting me. Either way, it unsettled Beau. Liam had to tell him we were fine, scratching his head, squeezing his paw, telling him, "It's all good, boy. We're okay."

We are okay. We're better than okay. I told Liam I loved him, and his reaction was visceral. He pulled me tighter, held me closer. We made love more intimately. Our kisses lingered longer, went deeper. Everything became less guarded, less tentative, more enduring.

As Liam shows Beau out the balcony door, I pull on a blousy pair of spun silk pajama bottoms and a t-shirt and find my way to the coffee. The service is set out on the dining table by a wide picture window overlooking the rising sun and the water below us. There must be twenty pleasure craft moored in the harbor. It's a favorite spot of island hoppers and sightseeing charters, as well as the yachting set. Somewhere out there is my boat, but I'm not sure which one it is. I had it brought out of dry dock for our visit. Hopefully we'll get a chance to take it out and do a little exploring.

With two cups of coffee in hand I make my way outside and to Liam who's watching Beau sniff around the shrubbery.

"Here you go," I nudge, handing him his cup of coffee, admiring the fact that he has zero insecurity about his body. He came outside wearing only his boxers. I adore the view. You'd have to be dead not to. Except for the fading scars on his right knee, he looks just like an overly-tattooed fitness model with a deeply chiseled six-pack and v-cut so pronounced it's damn near obscene. His biceps, chest, and lats so perfectly defined they look more like a statue of a mythical Roman gladiator than a real man in flesh and blood.

Flesh and blood are just what Liam is however, and he's all mine.

"I've got some friends that live here on the island," I mention casually, broaching the subject I've wanted to bring up since we got here. "I was thinking we could wander back to Mead Cay and spend the evening there. We could meet them, have dinner, go out for drinks, and maybe some dancing."

Liam sips his coffee, smirking. "You mentioned something about that last night as you were drifting off," he says, surprising me. I have no recollection of it.

"I did?" I ask, shocked. "What did I say?"

He shrugs. "Just that you had someone you wanted me to meet, a good friend."

'A good friend?'

"He's a good friend now," I say, feeling the need to disclose it all. "We were a couple for a few years. I still care about him—as a friend. We keep in touch."

Liam nods, not looking at me. Instead he keeps his focus on Beau, watching him wander the lawn, looking for the perfect spot to leave his morning deposit.

"We met in college. He's from here," I tell Liam. "He owns a restaurant and bar at the Cay."

Liam has no response.

"Are you okay with that?" I ask. "I'd just like for the two of you to meet. He knows about you, and I just…"

Liam turns to me, a sharp question in his eye.

"How does he know about me?" he asks. "You've never mentioned him, or anyone else to me before? How does he know about me?"

Sometimes he's just so dense. I reach forward, wrapping my pinky finger around his, swinging our hands to and fro.

"Because I've loved you… for a long time. Always," I remind him. "Because when I broke up with Marc, I felt like I owed him an explanation as to why it wasn't ever going to work. It was because I was already in love with you. I had to tell him that—tell him about you."

"Jesus…" Liam mumbles, his eyes misting. He looks away briefly, then back at me. Then he takes me inside his embrace, holding me tight like I might take flight and he needs to prevent it. "I thought maybe you were just talking in your sleep. I thought maybe I was imagining things."

"You're not imagining anything," I reassure him, sliding my one free hand up his back, trying not to spill coffee on him. "I love you, and I want to show you off to Marc and his friends, some of whom are also my friends. I want you to meet them."

Liam nods, standing back, wiping his eyes nervously. He calls Beau to heel at his side.

"I don't…" he says, "I don't know what to say, or how… how to act." He swallows hard, pushing more tears away. "Damn, Grayson. My family life was so fucked up. I don't think anybody's ever said those words before." He slips his hand down, anxiously stroking Beau's scruff. "I don't know what to do with it."

Now I might cry. My throat threatens to close. My eyes sting. This is half the reason I love him so much. He's just so easy to read. He's incapable of hiding anything. He's an open book and a good read, at that.

"Just accept it," I whisper, drawing near, placing my hand on his at Beau's nape. I lay my head in the crook of his shoulder and I whisper, "And find your way to loving me too, when you can. I'll wait. I've waited this long. I'll wait as long as it takes.

Liam lets go of Beau, and he brings me into an embrace. "I'm scared," he admits, pushing me back so we're face to face and eye to eye. "I'm scared to death of caring too much. Everything I care about goes away. Everyone I care about ditches me."

"Not me," I say, reaching up to touch his full, liquid lips with my finger. "I'm not going anywhere, baby. And I'm doing my dead level best to make sure you don't want me to." I smile at him, arching my brows in question. "What can I do to make you so happy, so contented with us, you never want to be anywhere except with me?"

Liam shakes his head, his beautiful blue eyes blinking. "Nothing," he says. "Nothing at all. I'm already there. There's nowhere else I want to be. Nobody else who matters a whit to me. It's just you. Just you."

Good.

* * *

MARC FONTAINE LIVED four doors down in the same residence hall as Tony and me. I remember the first time I saw him. He was barely eighteen years old, skinny like most boys his age, dressed in ridiculously baggy jeans and a Peter Tosh t-shirt. His skin was the same glowing hue as cinnamon toast, but his eyes were the color of coral growing on an ocean reef. His curly brown hair was cropped short, but concealed beneath this crazy knit Rasta cap that, at first blush, made you think he had a pile of dreadlocks concealed inside.

I only learned later that he had dreads before he came to MIT, but his father and mother made him cut them off in the erroneous belief that he'd be more easily accepted without them. They were wrong, of course, because everyone wanted to know Marc. He was beautiful, funny, and fearless the way few of us were fearless in those early days at school.

I'd go so far as to say I learned everything I know about fearlessness from Marc. I still love him, just not quite the way he always wanted me to.

He learned everything he would ever know about electromagnetism and electronics from me. Somewhere in between, we discovered what sex looked and felt like. We experimented, came out together, and cultivated a circle of friends that has persisted over the years. Marc and I were never really 'in love,' but there was always plenty of love between us. He was hurt when I broke it off. He asked if there was someone else, expecting me to tell him I'd met someone new.

Instead, I told him about Liam. We spent an entire night together, just talking about how much Liam meant to me, with Marc listening, enrapt.

"If you ever get together with this guy," he says. "I want to meet him. The one who's had your heart since junior high. I want to either shake his hand or punch him in the stomach."

"You better shake his hand," I told Marc. "Remember, he's a star quarterback and a badass. He'd stomp you into the AstroTurf."

That was a long time ago. I have little doubt Liam can still hold his own, but he's not nearly the badass he used to be. Today, he's truly reserved. He'd more likely walk away from a fight than ever seriously engage with one - even one defending his own honor.

Liam – who hasn't given a second thought to anything he's wearing since the first night we reconnected in Abingdon – has been lingering in the closet longer than usual. We bought a lot of new clothes yesterday, but he was half-hearted about it. I don't think he thought we might have somewhere to go that he'd want to dress for.

I come around the corner into the dressing room and am stopped in my tracks by a vision of Liam legitimately dressed. He's turned out in a pair of white linen slacks, rolled at the ankles. He's paired them with a powder blue linen shirt, half tucked, sleeves rolled up, brown penny loafers, and no socks. His belt is one of mine: woven brown leather with an understated silver buckle. He looks like he just stepped off a runway. That's always the impression he gives off.

"You look nice," I say, coming up behind him, peering into the mirror with him. "You clean up well."

He gives me a crooked smile. "Somebody bought me some styling threads. I thought I should put them to use since we're going to meet his ex. I don't want the guy to get any ideas."

I slip my hand around Liam's waist. "Who's this sugar daddy buying you swank clothes?" I ask, pulling him near. "I need to have a word with him."

Liam parts his lips, meeting mine. He kisses me, smiling into it.

"You look pretty good too," he says, coming back up after nipping my lips. "Then again, you always do."

A compliment! The man of few words finally springs for a compliment.

"Thank you," I say, checking myself out in the floor-length mirror. My outfit is a lot more casual: denim jeans, a tight black t-shirt, brown Red Wing boots, and my favorite

Tag Hauer watch. I like casual. I've spent enough of my life in suits. I'm done with that shit.

"You need a watch," I observe to Liam. "It's a critical accessory. People—shallow people we want to intimidate— judge you by your watch. Let's put a watch on that arm."

Liam laughs, smoothing out his shirt and sitting on the floor to play a quick game of fetch with Beau. "You are absolutely ridiculous. I give zero fucks about watches. And I've lived years not caring what time it is."

"Well, I'll lend you one. You can see how you like it."

Liam tosses a green Kong ball across the hardwood floors, and Beau scrambles after it. "Whatever you say, Gray. I did always want a nice watch back when I was in high school. It was just something I couldn't even consider in the past few years."

"I know." I go to the drawer on the far end of the closet where the watches are kept. (Hill brought my collection from home.) I run my eyes over them, considering each one, trying to decide.

Liam looks up at me, watching me with a scrutinizing eye. He lifts an eyebrow and makes some continued scoffing noises. But after a few moments, he stands up, putting his arm around my waist and pressing his lips to my neck. "That's nice," he says, peeking over my shoulder, pointing at one.

"You have exceptional taste. But I already knew that." I grin. He's chosen the Patek-Philippe Grand Complication 5327G with the perpetual calendar. In white gold and cobalt, it matches his outfit perfectly. But at a quarter million dollars, too many people would know it's borrowed. I want them to see Liam for who he is—talented, intelligent, kind, funny. I need *exactly* the right watch to convey that image, one that someone might guess he got for himself.

"It is nice," I say, "For another time. Maybe I'll get you one of your very own, just like it. I have something else in mind for you. Perfect for your personality."

"Watches don't have personality. But I gotta hand it to you, Gray. You have quite the insane collection."

"I do. And here's one that has your name all over it." I lift my Tudor Pelagos, a sturdy diver's watch with a titanium and steel case, from the box. It's the right heft and size for Liam's stature and build. It's the perfect color combination, cobalt blue and tungsten carbide, matching his outfit and his eyes perfectly. It's not a stupidly expensive watch. It's practical and beautiful, like Liam.

He leans his head on my shoulder. "I like it."

"Good," I say, taking his wrist. I slide it over his sturdy, still calloused hand, securing the clasp carefully... lovingly. "That's your watch. You should keep it. It's your first really good timepiece."

Liam looks it over, rolling his wrist, feeling the weight of it. He nods approvingly. "I won't keep it, but I'll borrow it," he says, halfway smirking. "It's pretty incredible."

"Please keep it," I say, lifting his hand and kissing his fingers. "It's perfect for you."

He rolls his eyes dramatically. "You know, I never wanted to be a kept man. I never wanted a life like this. Just something simple and good. A house and my dog. A truck, a good set of tools. I didn't need a watch, too."

"Well, I'd like to add a few other things to that mix, from time to time."

Liam nods and leans into me, kissing me long and deep. The day is brilliant and blue, all sunshine and salty air.

I would spend the rest of my life finding perfect gifts for Liam Gold if I could. I hope he'll let me try.

CHAPTER SIXTEEN

LIAM

I'm either falling head over heels for Grayson, or I'm the worst 'ho' on planet Earth. I'm going for the former because the latter has never been my modus operandi. Neither has getting all spiffed up and going 'out on the town', which is apparently what we're doing.

The restaurant Liam's taken us is packed with tourists and locals in equal parts. Management showed some foresight in the design of the place, however, in that the tourists come in the front door—the one facing the boardwalk and the ocean—and they have the bar and dining room at the front of the house to themselves. The back of the house, which opens onto a side ally with no view of the water, is just as large, but cozier. The bar here is loud, rambunctious, and the patrons seem altogether more relaxed and at home in their surroundings.

Liam leads me through the crowd like he's done this dozens of times before, so I assume he has.

A moment later a bartender recognizes him, nodding, calling out, "Ya! Grayson! My man! What the hell are you doing here?"

He's got a Brooklyn brogue that's weirdly out of place in this environment. A moment after seeing Grayson, he puts down his glasses of beer and comes forward to offer a hug.

I'm introduced to this man first, then another employee. Both welcome me warmly, but don't seem particularly intrigued by my presence. I guess Liam's brought people here before? Or maybe they're just polite.

"Marcus is around here somewhere," the bartender says. "Probably glad-handing his way across the front room, making sure we make payroll." He smirks at me, shrugging. "He'll be around in a few. What can I get you two?"

Before my rum and Coke is on the deck, Marcus appears with great fanfare.

"A little bird *told* me you were here!" he croons in a honey-tinged voice sweet enough for a boys' choir. He wraps Grayson up in a big bear hug, grinning from ear to ear as he does it. "You been gone a year, bro. You work too damn much! What finally got you back out here? Huh?"

"It was time I came back, that's all. And I have someone I want you to meet." A moment later I find myself the center of attention.

"Oh yeah?" His golden brown eyes size me up, and he gives me a generous smile.

"Marc, this is Liam Gold," Grayson says, drawing me forward, his eyes peering up at me proudly, like I'm a trophy he just won. "Liam, this is my dear old friend, Marc Fontaine."

"Holy shit!" Marc blurts out, looking up at me with a combination of wonder and doubt. "*The* Liam? The football player?" His accent is as lilting and soft as the sea, perfectly at home in this gorgeous place.

"In the flesh," I respond, putting my hand out.

It's irksome just how attractive and self-assured Marc is. He's got the confidence of a rock star or a Hollywood actor.

He's got presence, despite his small stature and slight build. He was born to wear that dapper, silk suit he's holding up like a coat-hanger, the wide shoulders of the jacket sliding casually off his, the fitted pants slung low, barely hanging on to impossibly narrow, boyish hips.

"And the flesh is something to behold," Marc states, taking my hand in his, turning my palm down. He places his other hand on top of mine, holding it between his. He stares up into my eyes, unblinking. "My good lord, you're so damn easy to look at. You need to come sit down over here with me."

The color rushes to my face. A hot flush makes my shoulder blades sweat. In another life, I'd be talking to this man in a heartbeat.

"Shameless flirt," Grayson quips, popping Marc's hands off mine dramatically. "Mitts off. You keep your hands to yourself."

Marc laughs, the sound melodic. That's how our night begins: with bawdy flirtation and smackdowns.

Marc invites us to a private room upstairs where we join a half dozen other men—all friends of Marc's and at least acquaintances of Grayson's—for a meal and socializing. They're flirty, happy, and as easy-going as any group of people I've ever been near. Grayson just blooms in their company, coming completely alive in a way he rarely is except when we're alone and intimate.

Over the course of a couple hours, I learn that Grayson came to Anguilla with Marc one spring break and he fell in love with the island. When he was able, he backed Marc in opening the restaurant, which has done very well.

"I've got thirty-five full-time, regular employees," Marc boasts between shots of Irish whiskey. "That's thirty-five jobs reserved for locals who probably wouldn't be be employed without Grayson."

"And more, with the good you do with this restaurant. Keeps tourists active on this part of the island."

Marc shrugs like he had absolutely nothing to do with it. There's still a glint in his eye when he looks at Liam, but perhaps that's just one successful businessman to another.

I learn that Grayson has helped others too. All these guys would extoll the long list of Grayson's virtues until he tells them to be quiet. "Give it a rest!" he admonishes. "If anybody wanted to hear that nonsense, they'd read my Forbes listing."

I read his Forbes listing. It didn't mention any of this.

All the men boo and hiss, waving off the notion.

"Are we going out?" one of the men asks, throwing down his linen napkin. "I want to do karaoke and dance!"

'Out' for this crew is a charted taxi ferry across the water to Saint-Martin, just seven miles south of Anguilla, to a strip of night clubs just off the Rue de la Liberté in the resort town of Marigot. It's disconcerting just how quickly you can move from one country to another here in the Caribbean, with no one in authority giving it any notice at all.

Anguilla is a territory of the British West Indies, so English is the official language. At Saint-Martin, the language is French. Disembarking the ferry with Grayson, his friends, and a dozen other tourists, I find myself slightly untethered. I can't read the street signs. I can't read anything.

"What the hell," I comment, laughing.

"Marc will get us around. We're not going far." Grayson takes my hand in his and pulls me in for a quick kiss.

Marc falls in beside me, while the others lead us through the narrow village streets. Looking around, it's clear to me that despite the fact that this place is geared toward well-heeled tourists, we're the only gaggle of swaggering gay men rolling down the street. Our companions ahead hang on one another, laughing, flirting, making no attempt to conceal anything.

Passersby glance at us, cutting their eyes—some with overt disapproval.

I look down at Grayson's hand inside mine, and anxiety swirls in my stomach.

"Relax," Marc says to me, noting my discomfort. "It's true there's a Catholic church on every corner here, but we own the night, and we own this street up ahead."

As it turns out, Marc is right. The street he refers to is just an ally way off the *Reu de Anguille*, but its old-world cobblestones are literally painted lavender. Both sides of the lane are lined with bars and restaurants, all packed to overflowing with people like us: men, women, and a few I wouldn't venture to guess which gender they started with. The music is loud and pumping. There's a band playing at the head of the street with an area roped off and dozens of couples dancing. Behind that are tables, and people sitting on and lounging by the low stone walls that line the ally. They're eating food, drinking, smoking, talking, basically having a grand time.

It's like photographs I've seen of The Castro in San Francisco. I've never seen an entire gay neighborhood in person before. This is a first. I can't help but smile broadly.

"*Mon amie!*" a voice calls as we pass. He reaches out, grabbing my sleeve, turning me around. "*Vous êtes belle! Viens t'asseoir avec moi!*"

He's a thirty-five (or so) year old man dressed in an expensive suit, smoking a long black cigarette, wearing Gucci glasses, grinning at me through an alcohol blur. I have no idea what he's said, but Marc laughs, pressing his hand to the man's chest, gently sitting him back down in his wrought iron chair.

"*Non, mon ami. Il a parlé pour,*" Marc says, shaking his head, wagging his finger at the man.

Grayson squeezes my hand tighter, giving me a tight

smile, biting his lip. "I'm going to need to keep an eye on you or one of these guys will steal you right out from under me."

Not likely.

"What the hell did he say?" I laugh. The night is warm and breezy, the ocean clapping against the sand in the distance.

"He said you're beautiful, and he'd like you to come with him," Marc says. "Can't say I blame him."

"Definitely not," Gray laughs. "I'll have to keep holding your hand."

I squeeze his hand. "I'm not going anywhere," I say, breathing it into his neck, pulling him to me. "I'm just along for the ride. I haven't been out for a night of fun... since college. It's been too long."

We eat, drink, dance, and play until the wee hours of the morning, surrounded by hundreds of others who've come from all over to do exactly the same thing. Marc and his friends have no inhibitions about being out in public, and neither does Grayson. I'm shocked when people start snapping photos of the party and Grayson goes right along with it, mugging it up with his friends without a single regard for where those photographs might wind up or who might have something to say about them.

When I was playing football, it would have been a career-ending mistake to wind up in a place like this and being seen with openly gay men. I learned quickly to keep myself in check and never make the mistake of being too forward, no matter who I was with or where I went, even if I knew I was among friends.

Grayson is completely unconcerned—I guess that's what money does. He doesn't care what others may think or how they'll perceive him. His value is measured by what he's built, not by who he sleeps with. He doesn't need to mollify 'fans.' He needs to satisfy shareholders. I guess the shareholders are less concerned with his sexuality than they are with his product development.

"Liam! Come get in here!" Andre, one of Marc's friends calls out. They'll all posing ridiculously with fancy, fruity drinks. And they're all getting more and more drunk.

Grayson pulls me into the photograph, wrapping his arm around my neck from behind, pushing me forward.

"You're so shy," he whispers in my ear. "I'm so proud of you. I want everybody to see how beautiful my boyfriend is." He presses his lips to my jaw, grinding his hips against me. "How did you manage to stay free so long?"

Grayson's more than a little drunk, so now I'm the one taking care of him. It isn't hard to do, as we're among friends in a friendly place. After all the alcohol is drunk and the bar lights go up, the restaurants shutter, and the music quiets. The first trailing lights of dawn appear in the sky. Our crew —still giddy, still laughing—makes its way through quiet, twilight streets to the ferry landing to await the first taxi back to Anguilla.

Grayson nods on my shoulder, dozing off, while I reflect on how we've spent our time.

He's built a company, made friends, lived out in the world unapologetically. I managed to make a royal mess of my world. When I got hurt, I shut down. I shut myself off from everyone who cared about me, closing myself away from everything.

Grayson came to see me in the hospital and I turned him away.

I could have made a different choice that day. I could have reached out and let him help me stand up on my own two feet again, but I was afraid.

"I love you," Grayson mumbles through hazy, alcohol fed sleep. We're parked on a bench by the waterfront, and I'm watching the sun come up while we wait for the first ferry of the day to appear. Marc and his crew lounge nearby. Someone has gone in search of coffee and we're all hopeful he'll return with a tray of steaming, frothy, lattes.

"I love you too," I admit to Grayson's sleeping form, finally willing to let my fear and self-doubt go. I pull Grayson closer, tucking him under my arm, kissing the top of his lovely head. "So much. And it's feels so good to finally be with you."

CHAPTER SEVENTEEN

GRAYSON

"*G*rayson, wake up, baby," a soft voice whispers in my ear. I love that voice, but I want it to be quiet, *just for now*. My head hurts. I need sleep. I'm old, and I didn't drink enough water last night.

"Come on," he says, not going away. "I've got coffee, water, and some Advil for you."

Coffee... That's what I need. *Advil?* I need that too. Whoever thought of all that is a *genius*. It's Liam. Of course, he *is* a genius. And he knows exactly what I need. I'm *so fucking glad* he's here. I manage a weak smile, but I don't open my eyes.

"Coffee?" I hear myself mumble through the dense blur of a hangover.

What did we do? How did I get here? I open my eyes, whining against the blinding, mid-day sun.

"Close the fucking blinds," I grumble, covering my head with pillows. "Fuck!"

The light is painful.

"Drake isn't happy," I hear Hill say. "Of course, he's never happy."

Drake? What's my hangover got to do with Drake? He's on vacation. I gave him the month off so I could get out from under his over protective, mother-hen rules.

"I closed the blinds," Liam assures me, laying his hand on my shoulder. "Now wake up and quit fucking around. We need you coherent."

I don't recall hearing that kind of urgency in Liam's tone before. *Something's wrong...*

Opening my eyes again, I sit up fast, almost involuntarily. My reaction is more like a reflex than anything else. My brain suddenly explodes, neurons firing at light speed. There's a thousand different things going through my head at once, from a flood of memories of last night's debauchery, to the idea that Drake's name shouldn't be on anyone's tongue right now; he should be on the west coast, drinking with his buddies *or something*.

Liam shoves a steaming, magnificently scented cup of coffee into my hand.

"Drink," he says. I do as I am told.

I hear the house phone ringing. Someone downstairs answers it. Mrs. Hill and Liam are both here with me, watching me sip coffee while I blink bleary sleep from my head. The cobwebs in my brain are thick and sticky, clogging my thoughts, obscuring my recollection.

I only have flashes of what we did last night after leaving Marc's restaurant. I remember the ferry to Saint-Martin, but after that it's a fog of snapshot pretty boys, dancing under lights, stumbling down cobblestone streets, and hanging onto Liam for dear life. I'm not used to drinking, and when I do, this sometimes happens. This is why I don't often drink. And when I do, I generally do it at home. I have zero tolerance.

"What happened?" I ask, almost afraid to know.

Hill looks at me like I'm a fragile flower. Liam's expression is loaded with concern.

"What happened?" I ask again, my worry increasing. "Why are you talking about Drake?"

"He's on his way here," Hill tells me. "With a full security detail. And Tony is coming too."

What the hell?

"What happened?" I ask again, this time the insistence in my tone breaking through. "What the fuck is going on?"

"This," Liam says, sliding his laptop opened to London's *Daily Mail* in front of me on the bed. "I didn't even see them, but they must have been following us."

The headline reads, *Tech Billionaire Grayson Ellis Slumming in Caribbean Hideaway with Gold Digger Boy Toy.*

The photos are as tasteless as they are invasive. They're shot from a good distance away, using a long lens. It's clear by the locations and variety of situations depicted in the collection of images, the photographer—or photographers—followed us around for at least two days. There are images of Liam and me getting cozy in the pool here at this house, then of us moving inside, arm in arm. There are a ton of images of us partying with Marc and his friends, us on the ferry drinking, and dancing, and more partying at the club on Saint-Martin. The clinchers though, are the shots of me passed out on Liam's lap napping on what looks like a park bench while he sips coffee and reads the paper.

None of this is all that bad. I look up at Hill and Liam, asking, "Is that all there is?"

Liam rolls his eyes, exhaling hard. "Read the article, Grayson," he says. "Read what they say."

I don't care what they say. "Liam, the *Daily Mail* is the worst fake news rag on the planet, and everyone knows…"

"Not everyone," Liam corrects, his tone rigid. He sighs. "Not the people who believe it, word for word. Read it. I'm smart enough to know that there are way too many people out there who take this shit *very* seriously."

I begin at the beginning, scanning each line. Nothing is interesting until I get four paragraphs down where the author mentions Liam's name, calling him, *'...a failed American footballer and a college dropout whose last known address was a rusting pick-up truck he frequently parked at the Walmart Supercenter in his hometown of Abingdon, Virginia.'* The reporter doesn't mention that Liam and I have known one another since childhood, but somehow she figured out he's the contractor on the renovation at Abingdon.

'Mr. Gold apparently worked his handyman magic, convincing the charming and handsome billionaire to fly the couple to Anguilla for days of high-end shopping and endless partying in Saint-Martin's infamous gay district.'

The author goes on, speculating about Liam's motivations, suggesting that due to my relative youth, I'm too easy to manipulate and am being taken to the cleaners by this *'parasite'* of a con man. Little do they know that I was the one looking for Liam. Idiots.

"What a load of rubbish," I mutter. "I'll sue the fuck out of them."

Liam stands up, his palms rising to his temples in the universal signal for *'I'm freaking out with anxiety.'*

"Tony's on his way here," Liam says. "He's livid. And your security guy, Drake, is coming too. He's freaking out, screaming at people on the phone."

"Who did he scream at?" I ask.

"Me," Hill replies. "Mostly me. Don't worry about it. I can handle it."

He's got no right. Then again, I did ditch him and lie to him about what I was doing. And now that those pictures and that story are out...

"The paparazzi are circling around this place like

vultures," Liam says, still pacing around the bedroom. "This is all my fault. I never should have…"

"Liam, don't be ridiculous," I say, holding my hand out to him. *I need that Advil he promised.* "I don't care what some tabloid says about us. We know this is all bullshit. That's all that matters."

I'd love the opportunity to prove that truth to him, but as soon as I finish my sentence, my phone – which someone miraculously placed on the nightstand, charging – rings. The ringtone is a special one I set up just for Justin Trivet's cell number so, no matter what, I'd always take his calls.

"I'm sorry, I've got to take this. It's Justin from Nicolai," I say, rolling over in bed to grab the phone.

"Justin, good morning," I answer, trying my best not to sound hungover or like I just woke up.

"Good morning," the familiar voice replies. "You sound awfully chipper for a man whose personal life just got dragged across the front pages of every scandal sheet on the planet."

It's more than just the Daily Mail?

"I'm ignoring it," I quip. "I'm sure they'll have someone even more entertaining to pick on tomorrow. You know nobody reads that stuff."

"Oh, how I wish that was true, but sadly, it's not."

Apparently, the stock markets respond to CEOs showing up drunk on scandal sheets passing out drunk with their gay lover.

"I asked you to lay low," Justin says. "Not fall in the gutter."

Our share price is down seven percent on the news, which has adversely affected our valuation for the merger.

"My team is balking at the asking price, given the drop in the company's value," Justin says. "I can hardly ask them to agree to pay that much more than the company is worth."

This is terrible news.

"Justin, this was a done deal. I don't understand," I protest. "We both signed letters of intent. We were just waiting for the final contracts to be drafted."

"And circumstances have changed," he states, his tone firm. "We'll be back in touch in a day or two to discuss new terms. In the meantime, try behaving like a CEO. Keep your boyfriend indoors or, better yet, send him home. You need to do some PR work to try to rehab your reputation. You're coming off as a queer frat boy: all entitlement and bad behavior with a kinky twist. It's not a good combo."

"Goddammit. It's my right to do whatever the hell I want. I'm not a child—"

"But you do have a company."

I groan and close my eyes against the building headache squeezing the front of my brain, and against the light, which aggravates everything.

"I'll stay tuned to hear from my lawyers," I say coolly. "I'm guessing your team has already been in contact with them, so they know this is coming?"

"Of course," Justin says easily. "The lawyers read the papers too. They saw this coming from a mile away."

Great.

I spend the rest of the morning on the phone with the board of directors, assuring them I'm neither on a bender nor under the Svengali-like influence of some gigolo. They don't care that Liam's been in my life since junior-high school. All they care about is hearing my voice and getting drunk on all that optimism I spew their way.

Before I can get back to Liam, to reassure him again that everything is going to be fine, I hear a commotion arise from downstairs.

The temporary security detail hired (over the phone, from L.A.) by Drake to see to my well-being, seems to have apprehended someone hell-bent on doing me harm. Either that, or Tony is downstairs going off on the poor guys for no reason at all.

"I'm the god damned CEO," Tony hisses at one of the guys set up in a free room just off the main kitchen on the ground floor. Behind me, the kitchen is a hive of activity, with Chef busy preparing something and half a dozen other staff walking here and there.

"Sir, there's no need to swear," one of the guys replies. "I just need some identification."

"It's okay," I say, coming into the room. "He's cool. He's with me."

For just a brief, fleeting, fleck of a moment, Tony appears relieved to see me. But before he can adequately blink away that tiny speck of vulnerability, his entire demeanor changes from one of anger with the security detail, to one of outraged fury—all aimed at me.

"You're selling the damn company," he tosses out at me like it's an insult. "You've had our corporate attorneys working on it for months, and you didn't think that was something I needed to know or be involved in? You're keeping secrets about the company from me, of all people? After all we've been through?"

"Slow down," I insist, holding up my hand. "This isn't personal. It was always about keeping it under wraps until it was done. It was always about controlling share value. I needed to keep it quiet, so no one ran up the stock price."

"Well now they're running it down," Tony observes, a smug smile cutting across his face. "So, how's all the cloak and dagger working out for you? Huh?"

I could punch him in the face. Or I could just pull rank and tell him to get out. Neither of those options seem particularly wise, and wise is what I really need to be right now.

"Did you come here with any solutions?" I ask. "Or did you just come to bust my balls? Because now that you're in on the merger deal, I could really use your ideas rather than just having you give me shit."

Tony uncrosses his arms, leaning forward, gripping the back of my office chair.

"I have ideas," he assures me, his eyes narrowing, pupils sharpening to dots. "I also have our public relations and social media people working on a strategy as we speak, but you're not going to like any of it."

Tony's wheels have been turning since he left home. I have no doubt whatever he's come up with in his mean little mind to turn this catastrophe around will probably work, but how many souls have to be sacrificed to make it so? Tony has a way of spreading fear and loathing wherever he goes.

"What ideas?" I ask him. "I'm listening."

CHAPTER EIGHTEEN

LIAM

"*Y*ou need to send that two-bit handyman back where he came from," Tony says. "I don't care how good he is on his knees. He's an epic liability who cost you about seventy million dollars this morning."

I hear Grayson arguing, loudly defending me. I hear the numbers concerning his current company's stock. I hear the shitty news about what this is doing to his reputation, to his entire world.

I hug Beau close, hoping to keep him quiet while I linger outside the door to Grayson's office. I'd intended to knock, telling them that lunch was ready, but when I heard Tony talking, I just couldn't help myself. I stood still, listening. Now I wish I hadn't.

"You're a global laughing stock," Tony goes on. "You're the punchline of every crude joke floating around every investment banking firm on Wall Street today. And your guys over at Nicolai? They're laughing all the way to the bank. They're going to screw you so hard on the acquisition price, you'll wish it was your boy Liam doing it. For all you know, they paid Liam to show when he did just so they could engineer a lower valuation under humiliating circumstances…"

I don't linger any longer. I pull Beau along by his collar, urging him to follow me back downstairs, back to the bedroom I've shared with Grayson over the last several days. Glancing around, I realize this room is all him and none of me. The clothes he bought for me, they were to impress his friends. The watch on my arm – which I remove and replace in the special box Grayson keeps them all in – is his selection for me. Hell, even the venue is all his choosing. *It's his magnificent house, his friends, his staff, his impression to make on me.* I'm reeling and disoriented.

I love Grayson Ellis, but there are so many reasons why this will never work. He's got a great big complicated life and I don't fit in it. None of his handlers want me in it.

Did I really cost him seventy million dollars? How? Just by being here?

Grayson was fine before we got together. Now everything he was working on is blowing up, and that's my fault. They're calling me a 'con man' and a 'boy toy'. They think I'm just here for the money.

I look up at the luxuriously furnished room, then beyond to the astounding view of the Caribbean. There's no way in hell I could ever get somewhere like this on my own. I could barely get across town without blowing a tire or running out of gas. Maybe they're right. Maybe I have just been hanging on Grayson's coat tails, taking advantage…

Beau looks up at me with a bewildered expression.

"I know boy," I say. "I'm sorry. I'll figure this out. I'm sorry."

I've never met this guy, Drake, that everyone seems so freaked out by. I don't think I want to. I think I've seen enough of what people really think of me.

Downstairs, I find one of the new security guys who showed up just after dawn this morning.

"I need some help," I say without preamble. "I'm pretty sure your boss wants me gone, so I'm hoping you can help me make that happen. I need to get a flight home, back to Virginia. Can you help me do that?"

The man—a hulking human in an ill-fitting suit—regards me curiously.

"Um, I guess," he says. "You serious?"

"Yeah," I reply. "As soon as possible. And I need to take Beau with me, so make sure I can bring him along."

"And Mr. Ellis is okay with this? He expressly wanted you to be here when he got out of his meeting." He looks at me and raises an eyebrow.

"Yeah, he okayed it. But also, I'm a human being as well. Just to be clear. This is my request, and I'd like you to help me fulfill it."

He shrugs. "Let me make a few calls."

I nod, handing him the American Express credit card Grayson got for me. "Use this," I tell him.

I have no other way to pay for the flight. I wish there was another choice. I'll return the card to Grayson and figure out how to repay him later. *This is for the best.*

Grayson's still with Tony when I go back upstairs, so instead of trying to speak with him about my decision, I just start packing. I don't have much to pack, as I didn't arrive here with any more than the old clothes on my back. I'm going to leave the things Grayson bought. When we were shopping, I didn't understand how other people would interpret it. I didn't realize they'd really think I was trying to score a payday. I wasn't. I just got caught up in Grayson's enthusiasm. It's easy to do that. *He's a sweet, generous, enthusiastic man with a huge heart.*

If I think too much, I'm going to fall apart. I can't afford to do that.

I just need to get home and figure out what's next. I need to figure out how to get out of Grayson's life so I don't ruin it. Everything I touch turns to absolute shit, and I won't bring him down into the muck with me.

In less than an hour, the security guy I spoke with appears with my card in hand.

"I booked you on a Delta nonstop to Atlanta with a layover and connecting flight to Roanoke," he says, handing my card to me. "You're going to need to leave here within a half an hour to catch the ferry to make the airport in time. They won't take your dog as a carry on though. You'll have to check him as baggage."

"What?" I say. "Baggage? What the hell?"

He shrugs. "I wouldn't do it. You hear horror stories of pups getting lost or, worse, getting loose. Nightmare."

I can't risk that. *No way.* As if he's reading my mind, Beau stands up, giving me a concerned expression in tandem with a low, guttural whine.

"It's okay buddy," I say. "I won't do that. You need to be safe, no matter what."

I shouldn't have brought him on this ill-conceived adventure. Hell, I shouldn't have brought myself. I should have stayed at home in Abingdon, in my own truck, in my place, right where I belong. I don't know what I was thinking trying to get outside where I have always fit in. I always do this and I always wind up getting beat down further than I started.

Grayson wouldn't let anything happen to Beau. I know he'll come back to Abingdon eventually, after the deal with Nicolai is done. He'll bring Beau home to me then.

I sit down at the small desk in the cozy sitting room just off our bedroom. There's a fancy note pad and a pen in the desk. I think for a moment about what to say and how to say it, then – once my thoughts are organized – I begin writing.

Grayson,

Before I offer an apology, I first need to beg for a favor. I'm leaving Beau in your hands and praying it's not too much to ask to keep him near you - to keep him safe, fed, and walked while you have him. When you come home to Abingdon, I'll collect him. The airline wouldn't let me take him on board and there was no way in hell I was going to check him as baggage through an Atlanta layover. I know you'll understand.

I apologize for bolting on you without explanation. I've heard and seen enough of all that's going on to know my presence here isn't helpful to you, and that it's deeply offensive to some. I hope you know I would never have caused you these problems if I'd had the brains enough to foresee what would happen. I am so sorry. I hope that once I'm gone, everyone realizes you're fine and I can't screw things up for you anymore.

You and I were a great idea that felt good in theory, but will never work in practice. We're from wildly different worlds. Your world is suspicious of me, with good reason. I love you. I believe you love me. But that's not enough to overcome all the obstacles. I won't be the thing that ruins everything for you.

When you get back to Abingdon, we'll figure out how to finish the house with the least amount of awkwardness possible. I can recommend some good people.

I hope everything works out with the merger. Again, I am so sorry to have caused all these problems for you.

All my love,

– Liam.

By the time Grayson finds my note and finds Beau curled up, sleeping at the foot of our made up bed, I'm thirty thousand feet in the air, watching a string of tiny Caribbean islands disappear over the misty horizon. A flight attendant hands me a plastic cup and a small bottle filled with brown liquid. It's the first time I've wanted to drink anything harder than a beer in a very long time. As far as I am concerned, she can keep these coming until the plane touches down.

I sip the sharp liquid, feeling Tony's words to Grayson like a solid rebuke against my character. He said dreadful things and he believed them. The papers said things. *How did the papers know I was working for Grayson? How did they know I was living in my truck? Did the tabloids send reporters to Abingdon? That seems unlikely. I wonder who talked to them?*

CHAPTER NINETEEN

GRAYSON

I look at the note, reading the words again. I still can't believe them.

"Gone?" I ask. "Gone how?"

Hill shakes her head. "I don't know," she says. "I can't even tell he's taken anything with him. Beau's under the bed. His clothes are folded up in the closet, most still in the shopping bags they came in. Even his shoes are in their boxes."

"Where could he go?" I ask again. "It's a bloody island!"

"Don't look a gift horse in the mouth," Tony offers, his eyebrows arching happily. "He's a resourceful character. He's smart, that boy. He probably booked a commercial flight."

"Obviously," I reply, annoyed. "But he probably didn't do it on his own. He doesn't know where the airport is. He doesn't know which carriers service it. I doubt it was even his idea to go..."

Tony throws up his hands. "Grayson! Who cares whose idea it was? If he's gone, then good riddance! He was an albatross around your..."

I've had it.

"Shut the fuck up!" I hurl at him, frightening Hill in the

process. She takes two steps back while Tony bows up, shocked that I'm coming at him fully loaded. "You fucking did this! I know you did. Nobody else would or could. You had the access, the knowledge, and the motivation. You..."

Tony shakes his head, raising his hand. "I did you a favor," he retorts angrily. "You're just too far up your own ass to see it. You'll thank me. That loser football player isn't good enough to clean your boots. He never was."

He really did do it. I can't believe it. But then again, I really can. He was angry from the moment Liam came back into my life. He started looking for a way to wreck everything and I gave him the perfect opportunity.

"Get out," I state calmly, lifting my phone. I text the security desk at Theos corporate headquarters in Mountain View.

"Grayson, think about this," he says, his tone dropping.

I text my executive code to the security desk, then quickly type the following instructions: *'Immediately terminate COO, Anthony Carraro. Close his network and VPN access, passwords, etc. Shut off his access to voicemail, company messaging, and facilities. Cancel his company credit cards, etc. If HR has questions, tell them to call me.'*

Once that's done, I turn to Hill.

"Mrs. Hill, can you bring one of the security guys up here, please?"

"Grayson, what the hell are you doing?" Tony asks, his tone imploring.

"Terminating your employment," I quip in response. "Removing you from my company and my life. Now get the fuck out of here."

"Grayson, calm down," he insists. "You're overreacting. This is crazy. After everything we've been through together? After everything we built?"

"We?" I repeat. "*We* didn't build this, Tony. *I* built this. It's *my* ideas, *my* patents, and *my* company. All you did was sell a brilliant idea into a marketplace starving for brilliant ideas that was willing to throw money at them. I could have hired any frat boy with a Rolodex to do that and had the same result. It seems like you didn't hear me before. So I'll repeat myself—get the *fuck* out of my house."

Tony's eyes darken to pitch black dots inside narrow slits. He's enraged, his anger still building.

"You'll regret this," he spits. "You're a fucking arrogant little shit with no gratitude, and you'll regret it."

A big, darkly tanned body guard wearing an Izod sport shirt and black cargo pants appears with Hill on his tail. He looks at me, then at Tony, and before either of us blink I see the recognition in his eyes. He lifts his hand, directing it toward Tony, then to the door.

"This way, Mr. Carraro," he says. "I'll see you out."

Tony clenches his jaw. "Grayson, don't do this," he says. "You're right. I shouldn't have sold him out, but I did it for you. He'll never be good enough for you. He'll never deserve you. Please Grayson, I'm begging you. It's always been about you and me. He was just a distraction you don't need. Let me show you…"

This has gone to a place I never anticipated. Never in a million years would I have imagined hearing words like those come from Tony Carraro's mouth. He's the antithesis of gay. He's toxically heterosexual and ridiculously macho. Or maybe that's just how he gets by? Why did he never let on before? Why didn't I see it? *Jesus, what did he think? That he and I would…?*

I nod at the patiently waiting security guy. "Get him out of my sight," I insist. "And get him off this island. His Anguilla privileges are cancelled."

"I swear to God," Tony hisses as my security guard ushers him out. "You'll regret this."

"I already regret the connection to you," I reply. "I wish I could go back in time and take it back."

Once the object of my ire is removed from my presence, I return to the original matter at hand.

"I want to go home to Abingdon," I say to Hill. "Can you organize that while I try to salvage this merger?"

She nods, pursing her lips. "Do you think you can fix things with Liam?"

The pressure of that question presses tight in my chest. I want to breathe, but it's almost painful to draw air.

"I don't know," I admit. "That's going to be up to Liam."

"He's not a gold digger," Hill says. "I know the type, and he doesn't fit it."

I nod, agreeing with her. "I know, but I'm not sure Liam's willing to take the accusations. He's been through a lot, and none of it good."

"Then we better do everything we can to make sure sticking around is a good option," she says. "And make sure he knows you don't believe any of that nonsense."

I wish I knew how to do that.

What I do know is that Liam's more important to me than money. I'll scrap the merger and rededicate myself to taking Theos to the next level if Liam is at my side. I'll do whatever I need to do to make him stay.

I thought I lost him forever. When I found him again, I never intended to let go. This time, I'm not going to let him slip away without a fight.

CHAPTER TWENTY

LIAM

*A*tlanta-Hartsfield International Airport is daunting, even to someone like me who spent three or four months of the year on the road with my college football team. I got to know the inside of almost every major airport in the country, but Atlanta is still a challenge. I drop my only bag on a chair under the table at a nondescript burger joint inside the Delta terminal and peer up at the menu. Suddenly, I'm longing for fresh crab crepes, blackened sea bass, or anything prepared by Grayson's attentive, talented chef. He's spoiled me.

That's over. Time to move on.

I order a bacon cheeseburger and fries, hoping for the best. These places are always hit or miss.

I hate airports. I always have. They're fake, depressing, and they smell like anxiety and greasy food. The only way people can tolerate them is by consuming greasy, salty, overly seasoned food and watching television from the stacked banks of screens dominating the interior design of every public space from waiting rooms to restaurants and bars.

I'm no different. I gnaw my burger, sip my beer, and peer up at the wide, colorful screen overhead. Ordinarily, I'd glance up then glance away because what's playing on a television mostly holds no interest for me, but just now my attention is seized.

"And this news just in at two hours before market close," a leggy, blond spokesmodel on Bloomberg TV says, beaming into the camera. "It's being reported by several insiders close to the management team at Theos Universal, the cutting-edge battery manufacturer that's breathed new life into the sustainable energy sector, that Grayson Ellis, the company's CEO, has engaged in merger negotiations with Nicolai Automotive, the largest all-electric vehicle maker in the world. While Theos is publicly traded, Ellis owns or controls a majority of outstanding shares, giving him near carte-blanche to do as he sees fit with the company he founded."

Below the pretty blond spokesmodel, a floating banner slowly scrolls by, quoting the current market prices of popular U.S. and global stocks. TEOS, the symbol for Grayson's company scrolls by. The value is down – sharply – since last week.

"In what appears to be related news, and an event impacting Theos' share price globally, is a rumor that CEO Ellis is involved with former college football star Liam Gold, whose professional football prospects were slapped down in a spectacular hit during bowl season almost ten years ago. Since then, Gold has drifted and is rumored to be homeless, possibly with substance abuse issues. Related to that, co-founder and Chief Operations Officer Tony Carraro has been forced out after a falling out with CEO Grayson Ellis over personal issues..."

What?!

My heart stops, skipping in my chest. A half-chewed ball of burger and bun sticks in the roof of my mouth.

What?!

Tony Carraro and Grayson don't always get along, but they've been together since college. They started the company together. *How could this happen? Why now? And what does it mean?*

The two of them have known one another almost as long as Grayson and I have known one another, with one big difference: there hasn't been a ten-year long gap in their relationship. What kind of falling out could cause a breach like this? Maybe Tony's the one behind leaking all this to the media and making up stories about me being a con artist *and now a drug user.*

It's entirely possible, but I'll probably never really know. Now that I've cut and run, I doubt Grayson includes me on any more top-secret dealings having to do with Theos or anything else.

Before I've finished my burger and beer, my flight is called. It's scheduled to be a little over an hour, nonstop flight to Roanoke, on a tiny, cramped plane without enough overhead bins. I manage to shove my bag in and get the thing closed when the lady across the aisle yells at me for hogging the bin. I open it back up and step back, giving her ample opportunity to attempt to fit more in there. But after too much whining and swearing on her part, I take my bag out, shove it under my seat between my feet, and hope the flight attendant doesn't notice.

I'm all strapped in, tucked into the narrow, uncomfortable seat when my phone starts ringing. It's in my ass pocket, which requires some impressive over and under acrobatic maneuvers in order to retrieve it before the call goes to voicemail.

Once I have the thing in hand, I see Grayson's number on the screen.

He's found the note.

"Hello?" I answer, feigning like I don't know who it is.

"Liam—" The line is noisy, billeting with the sound of a hurricane blowing a thousand miles per hour, accompanied by the roar of powerful engines.

"Grayson?"

"Where are you?" He asks, skipping the pleasantries. Despite the noise, he's all business. "I'm on my way to you. Just tell me where to come. Are you in Atlanta? You should be in Atlanta by now. Wait for me there."

"Don't, Grayson," I hear myself saying against the will of every cell in my body. "I'm a liability you don't need in your life."

"Fuck that," he hisses, the passion in his tone piqued. "I love you. Not another damn thing matters. Now tell me where you…"

The line drops out, leaving me cold.

I didn't even get a chance to ask about Beau, or see if he was okay--to make sure he was with Grayson, wherever Grayson is. I miss him. Hell, I miss both of them, but I have to believe I'm doing the right thing for Grayson. As for Beau, that's another story. We've never been apart, not since the first day I found him. I can't imagine what he's thinking: that I've left him forever? He must be heartbroken, but Grayson *will* bring him back to me. Beau and I will be together again soon and things will go back to the way they used to be before I got too big for my britches and forgot where I came from.

I never should have dragged Beau into this. I hope he's okay. I hope he's not scared.

CHAPTER TWENTY-ONE

GRAYSON

$\mathcal{D}$rake puts down his phone, peering at me with anxious reserve, shaking his head.

"Sorry, Mr. Ellis," he says. "Delta security says the plane departed on schedule with Mr. Gold on board."

Great. There is no intercepting him now. He's hours ahead of us and I still have a crisis I need to deal with.

I've been on the phone with my public relations and communications people since we got in the air. They're under instructions to get me an exclusive, live, on-air segment with either Bloomberg or CNN as soon as I'm on the ground. I thought that was going to happen at the airport in Atlanta. Now, I'm not sure where it'll be.

I dial my personal assistant, Naomi, for the latest information. She's sitting with the PR team in Mountain View.

She picks up instantly, before the first ring has even rung. She knows me well, knowing I don't like to waste time when I'm stressed out. She skips the pleasantries.

"You're booked for a ten minute segment on Bloomberg as soon as we get you on the ground and linked up. I have a room at the VIP lounge at Atlanta…"

"Atlanta's out," I inform her. "Liam's gone on to Roanoke. How about Miami?"

"Even better," Naomi quips. "Let me make some calls and I'll call you back. How long 'til you land there?"

"I don't know," I tell her. "I'll know when you call back."

I hit the button for the flight attendant as we end the call. When she appears, I ask her to pass along to the pilots my desire to alter our destination.

"We won't be on the ground long," I add. "As soon as I finish the T.V. segment, we're back in the air to Roanoke. Be sure to make that clear to them as well."

"Yes sir," she says, smiling and nodding formally. "Right away."

Drake's not even looking at me. He knows I'm just one step away from firing him and his entire team. It's one thing if Liam wanted to go, but they should have told me. Nobody gets to assume they know what's best for me. No one gets to interfere in my life without my cooperation. That goes for Drake and his team, and it goes for Tony too. He crossed a line and there's no forgiveness after that.

Tony has put things into motion that will take a miracle to undo. There's no coming back from a mistake like that. I don't care if we were friends. I don't care if he was a co-founder. He's history now. He assumed way too much.

Thinking about Tony and everything he's done to sabotage the merger, my relationship with Liam – just everything – is almost enough to send me into a spiral of anger. Almost, but not quite, because I've got a distraction and it won't let me sink into a bad mood and stay there long. Beau pouts, lifting his head high, then dropping it onto my thigh, looking up at me with big, sad, brown eyes. He's so pitiful – so forlorn without Liam – it's almost comic. He knows how to play it up.

"I promise," I tell him, reaching down, firmly scratch the

dense, fur covered flesh behind his ears. "We're on our way to him. You'll see him tonight if I have anything to do with it. I know I'm a sorry substitute."

Beau whimpers, never breaking eye contact with me. His expression is a mask of sadness and confusion. He doesn't understand where Liam is. He doesn't understand why he's been left behind with the likes of me.

* * *

THE MIAMI DADE airport does a huge business in charters and private jets coming and going from all over the world. They know how to treat a VIP. I barely have to walk five hundred steps from the plane to a private media room where an airport staff member is already busy setting up and testing the satellite link with New York. She and Hill run through a couple of drills while a stylist brought in at the last minute by my PR people gets me ready with a quick trim, some powder and color, and a clean, sky-blue shirt that'll look great on television.

She straightens my collar, squaring the shoulders, then stands back to have a look.

"Hot," she pronounces. "Hot AF."

That's good I guess because, as soon as I'm settled down in silence with a speaker in my ear and not another thing to think of, the Bloomberg financial show host comes on with a snarky observation about me looking pretty good for a guy who was out drinking all night long.

We're not on air yet and I know it, so I take this opportunity to remind him, "You know I can scrap this thing and take it across the street to CNN, right? They would absolutely *love* this story."

He changes his attitude, *post haste*.

"Pardon me, Mr. Ellis," he says. "I was just trying to lighten things up a bit. I know it's been a tense day for you."

"Not in the least," I lie. "I love a challenge."

An unseen producer speaks quietly into my earphone, informing me that we'll go live in ninety seconds. The small camera positioned in front of me powers up, a tiny light on its left side, blinking red. Naomi, my PA, is on the phone listening to everything. Hill is seated just a few paces away, quietly observing, providing moral support.

"You'll do great," Hill says, her voice soft. "Remember you don't have anything to prove to anyone."

Those are the precise words I needed to hear and focus on as the sound in my ear ramps up to the banter of the television show host talking about another company that's in the news today, announcing unexpected layoffs. A few seconds later the producer is back on, telling me we're going hot in ten seconds and I'll be introduced.

"Look directly into the camera," he says. "Try to smile. Keep it upbeat. Keep your hands down. Six. Five. Four…"

I've been on television dozens of times. These are instructions he shouldn't need to give me, nevertheless, I'm grateful for the reminder. It's easy to come off like an unstable, arrogant lunatic on television if you start waving your hands or scowling in response to a statement you don't agree with. Your best bet is always to nod and smile, then add a lengthy correction to clear up the bullshit you just smiled at.

"The scandal sheets were up early this morning with news of Theos Universal's CEO, the twenty-something billionaire Grayson Ellis, and allegations he's having an affair with a homeless ex-football player who some have character-ized as a con artist," the show host begins by way of intro-ducing me. "Meanwhile, Theos insiders are claiming that Ellis has fired co-founder and long-time COO Anthony Carraro after he confronted his boss on rumors that Ellis had been conducting secret merger talks with Nicolai Automotive.

"They say it's better to be talked about than ignored," he quips smugly, "So, we have Grayson Ellis live to address his very busy news day and respond to all these rumors and allegations. Mr. Ellis, can you tell us whether you'd rather be ignored or talked about today especially?"

That's my cue. I'm on. The world is watching. How I handle myself in the next five minutes will determine whether the merger goes south and whether or not I even have a company left after all the debris clears.

"I'd always rather be talked about," I reply, smiling. "There's really no such thing as bad press. It just creates another opportunity to get out there and show people what's really going on."

"Well how about you tell us what's going on?" he asks. "You're speaking with us from Miami? Is that right? I understand you've been in the Caribbean for several days. What's going on there?"

I smile, trying to look at ease. "I took my boyfriend on a small vacation while Theos' attorneys and Nicolai Automotive's attorneys worked out the fine print on the merger deal we've been negotiating for months. I've been trying very hard to keep the merger quiet, as leaks of that sort will affect stock prices. The best course of action seemed to be to make myself scarce from the office so my activities involved with the merger didn't tip anyone off."

"It looks like that strategy blew up on you," the show host says, his tone leaden with smugness. "Is it true Tony Carraro leaked details of the merger and your relationship with the former football player, Liam Gold, to the tabloids? Is that why you let him go?"

"Among other things," I concur. "I'm sure Mr. Carraro is already consulting with his attorneys, but let it suffice to say that whatever it costs me, it'll be a small price to pay to make Tony Carraro go away. His presence had become a toxic influence within the company."

"Ouch!" the amused host cries. "That sounds like an expensive break up! With your stock price down so low, are you sure you can afford it?"

I smile again. "It's only low because Tony tried to spread lies and innuendo about me, personally. Whatever my short-comings, they don't adversely affect the quality of Theos' offering. Our products are sound, our financials are stellar, and Nicolai has made an intelligent bid. I wish we'd been able to keep the merger quiet a bit longer, but it is what it is. I'm confident our share price will rebound *and then some* by the time the deal is finally struck."

We go on for a few more minutes just like this, and I'm hoping that's all there is going to be to it, when I'm caught off guard by the show host's last question.

"So, what's become of the football player?" he asks. "You said he was your boyfriend, but we've heard reports he left Anguilla earlier today and that you're traveling separately."

"That's true," I admit, then decide to pour it on thick. "Unfortunately, Liam – who's not as familiar or comfortable with the politics of running a company as I am – was blind-sided by the accusations made against him. He believed his presence was somehow materially damaging me, Theos, and our prospects at successfully completing the merger. He left, thinking he was doing the right thing. Of course, that's exactly what Tony Carraro hoped he'd do. It was always Tony's goal to drive him away. I think Tony had some unre-alistic expectations about where he fit in my life. I set him *straight* on all of those notions as I was firing him. Liam's not here to defend himself, so I'll do it for him. I've known Liam Gold since we were teenagers. We met in tenth grade. We were best friends in high school – more than that, really.

182

Liam's one of the best men I've ever had the privilege to know. He's a decent, hardworking soul who's rarely gotten any good breaks in his life. I love Liam, and I'm looking forward to seeing him as soon as I get home."

The camera goes dark a few seconds later and I hear the host thank me for coming, then move on to the next topic du jour. I take a deep breath, remove the mic from my shirt collar, the earphone from my ear, and look over at Hill. She is beaming.

"I told you you'd do great," she says. "You did wonderful."

Naomi seconds her assessment, then comments that the stock price bounced up a point during the interview.

"Let's keep an eye on it," I tell her. "I'm headed back to the plane and to Roanoke. I've gotta catch up to Liam and let him know he's no liability to me."

"Good luck," Naomi says. "We're rooting for you—and Liam. Let us know how it goes."

Fifteen minutes later we're airborne again and I'm stretched out with a hand on Beau's shoulder, reassuring him we're on our way to see his dad. He peers up at me with sad, dark eyes, as if to ask me if I really mean it.

"I really do," I tell him. "We'll be back with Liam in just a couple hours."

The idea that Liam left Beau in my care gives me hope that he hasn't completely given up on us. He loves this loyal animal more than he loves his own life. He must trust me if he left Beau with me, not knowing what my plans would ultimately be. He must believe in me, hoping I'll come after him.

CHAPTER TWENTY-TWO

LIAM

*I*n my entire life I've never been so happy to see dilapidated farm buildings and weathered, old oak trees. Landing in Roanoke – after days out in the exotic tropics in the Caribbean, then my day of tedious commercial air travel winding up in the sprawling excess of Atlanta's international hub – is a welcome homecoming. I don't need a map to find my way to baggage claim. I don't need directions to get me to the rental car desk. I don't even need GPS to get me "home" to Grayson's lake house. The familiarity of my surroundings is comforting. And for the first time in a long time, I feel safe after weeks of being in strange places with strange people, never knowing what's coming next. I like an adventure, but this one didn't end well.

It's good to be home.

The streets of Abingdon are quiet as I navigate through before heading south on Highway 75. It's late in the afternoon and the sun is inching down toward the mountaintops, allowing a chill to creep into the early autumn air. I missed the way the air smells: crisp and clean, dry, with a hint of apple and burned hickory.

I pass a city police officer sitting in his cruiser in the parking lot of the Chick-N-Little, watching cars roll by. He doesn't recognize me or my rental car, so he watches me carefully from behind shaded sunglasses. I almost expect him to pull out and follow because that's what he would do in my former life. Tonight, however, he turns his gaze back down the road, uninterested in me or my destination.

The sun is almost down and the house is completely dark by the time I arrive. I forgot just how forlorn this old place seems when no one's around. That lonesome feeling is part of what attracted me to it back when Grayson and I were kids. Even though people lived here, it always seemed almost neglected – *unloved* – like it was looking for someone to turn it into a home, not just a nice house.

Ordinarily, when I slip my key in the door and turn the lock, Beau comes bounding down the hall toward me, loping to a skidding stop at my feet, wagging his tail in greeting. Tonight, I'm met only by shadows and the persistent beeping of the security system, prompting me for a disarm code.

This house needs people and animals. It's too big and too quiet to be left to its own devices. I reach over, touching the switch on the wall and flipping it. The room brightens, but it's still lonely. The security system continues to sound its demand.

"I think I'll just check on things, then head over to my cabin," I say out loud to no one, slightly startled by how my voice carries along the high ceilings, echoing off the corners.

As much as I hate to admit it, I'm spooked by the lonely isolation of the house and its hidden spot on the lake. As a kid, I was enthralled with it. When Grayson and Beau are here, I love it. But right now, I'm a bit creeped out like someone's watching me. The hair on the back of my arms and my neck stands on end.

Just then, I hear steps on the porch directly behind me.

Reflexively, I spin around to meet the noise head on. I'm stunned to come face to face with Tony Carraro. He's come into the foyer just behind me, his hand still on the screened door, propping it halfway open so it doesn't squeak on closing.

He smiles at me. The smile is chilling, almost sinister.

"It's a little spooky out here in the dark," Tony observes coyly. "I have no idea why Grayson likes this place. So much of who he is is a mystery to me. I hope it won't always be like that."

What's he even talking about?

"What are you doing here, Tony?" I ask, thoroughly confused. "How did you even get here? I left before you did."

He nods, still smiling. "Yeah, but I chartered a private jet. Because I have money. You don't. Unless you used Grayson's?"

I don't respond.

"Where's that dog of yours?" he asks, looking around. "That's a serious looking dog."

"He's with Grayson," I say, wondering why he's interested in Beau. "Why?"

I turn away from him to touch the security panel at the other end of the hall, quickly punching in the code before the alarm sounds. The beeping stops. As I turn back to Tony, meaning to ask him again why he's here, my ears note the peculiar 'whooshing' sound of an object flying at a fast speed nearby. He's reared back, unwinding, swinging something large in my direction.

"Just 'cause," he replies. His eyes are bright, and his face flashes with inhuman rage. "Just 'cause I was wondering who might see me."

I hear a loud crack, see a blinding white light, and then feel a sharp pain rip between my ears.

The last thing I'm aware of, after everything has faded to

black, is the sound of my dog's frantic, angry barking and agitated growling. Something important happened, but I don't know – don't understand – what it is. Beau couldn't be here yet. Neither could Grayson. It's an illusion, a comforting one. I'll take it.

"C'mere boy," I hear myself saying as I land on the floor with a thwack. My throat tightens, and I cry out in pain. Lightning strikes inside my head, my conscious mind blurring with the imagined sounds of my dog in the distance. I can't open my eyes. I can't hear myself think for the ringing in my ears. I can't stand up; my body won't let me. There are other sensations, the sensation of being hit, again and again, but I barely feel it as the light in my head begins to flicker off.

It seems dangerous. It seems life-threatening, but I'm dreamy, distant, and euphoric. Finally, my brain fades. My last thoughts are of Beau and Grayson, and if I'll ever see either one of them again. I wonder if either of them know – could possibly know, since I left them like they were nothing to me at all – just how much I love them both.

If I had everything to do over again...

CHAPTER TWENTY-THREE

GRAYSON

"*W*ere you expecting any guests?" Drake asks me as we pull into the driveway, approaching the house.

Looking up from my tablet where I've been texting members of my public relations team, I see the car in the driveway. The lights are on in the house. The front door is wide open.

Beau stands up on all fours, pressing his nose to the window, looking out. He lets go with a low, guttural growl. The spiky hair on his back sticks straight up in the air, twitching like he's deeply agitated.

"It's Liam," I say. "He's here. He probably got a rental car."

I reach forward, resting my hand on Beau's shoulder. "It's okay, boy," I say. "You'll see him in a minute."

The dog shrugs my hand off, shifting his stance. He raises his big head, barking loudly, then digs deep into the leather seats with his hind legs, like a bull getting ready to charge.

"Beau, calm down," I urge. "It's okay."

We pull closer to the house and Beau's attitude does anything but calm. He's chomping at the bit to get out of the car, pawing the glass, standing on his hind legs, whining and growling.

"What's wrong, Beau?" I ask. Drake turns, looking back at the dog. Then, following Beau's line of sight, he moves his gaze to the open front door of the house.

"Stay in the car, sir," Drake instructs me. "The dog's reaction is making me nervous. I'd like to check it out first."

As soon as Drake opens his door, Beau bolts, leaping over the console, nearly knocking Drake down as he rolls past at a full-on gallop toward the porch. He's snarling, barking, and growling - all three at one time. I've never seen anything like it and, like Drake, it raises my alarm. There is no way in hell I'm staying in the car.

As soon as I'm on my feet, clear of the car, I hear Beau seize on something or someone. The sound of a ferocious canine attack is unmistakable. The gnashing of teeth and ripping of fabric and flesh have their own signature sound, as does the sound of the terrified man who finds himself the object of such an angry dog's outrage and aggression.

"Get him!" I hear someone scream as Drake bounds over the threshold. "Get him off me!!!"

The scream is frantic, desperate, wrenched with terror and pain.

Is Beau attacking Liam? Why would he? What's happening?

I take the front steps three at a time and make the porch in seconds flat. Just inside the front door, Drake lingers, almost frozen, trying to assess the situation.

Coming up behind him I see the blurry, violent tumble of dog and man wrestling for dominance, the dog clearly winning. Beyond them, another few yards inside, I see a figure lying sideways, legs splayed wide on the floor. His big frame, despite the fact that he's as limp as a rag doll, is familiar to me.

Then I see the blood.

There's blood everywhere. It's on his head and smeared across his face, on the floor in a growing pool beneath him, and soaked into his shirt at his chest and shoulder. The rug is likewise smeared with blood. There are large red welts on his arms. His shirt is half untucked. There's a boot print on the fabric of his jeans at his hip. More gray, dirty scuffs criss-cross Liam's shirt as if someone landed blows with their feet. There's a bloodied baseball bat on the floor rolling between the tumble of outraged dog, the object of its fury, and Liam's limp figure.

My hearts stops, then races forward. I taste bile on my tongue while rapidly piecing together what happened here.

"Stay back, sir," Drake insists, standing still himself.

"Call 911," I shout, shoving past him, past Beau, moving toward the spot where Liam lay on the floor, bleeding and unconscious.

"Get the fucking dog!" an all-too familiar voice cries between snarls and snaps of Beau's powerful jaws.

I couldn't care less if Beau rips his throat out. The knowledge that the object of Beau's assault is Tony briefly crosses my mind then just as quickly passes by. Let Beau have him. Let Beau solve *that* problem; I don't care what damage he does. I have to take care of Liam.

Liam is out cold, the blond hair on the side of his head a tangled, bloody mat. He's still bleeding. The collar and shoulder of his shirt is soaked. The floor and rug beneath him is too. I drop on my ass to the floor, lifting him in my arms, pulling him backwards onto me, his limp head flopping onto my chest.

"Oh God, baby, please be okay," I hear myself say as if I'm hearing my voice through a long tunnel.

I'm shaking, terrified. He's clammy to the touch. His skin is sticky. I reach up and touch his face, seeing his blood on my hands. I pull him tight against me, wrapping myself around him, trying to lift him onto my lap. He's completely limp and unresponsive. I touch his throat looking for a heartbeat. At first there's nothing, but then I find it. It's shallow but steady and rapid.

"Wake up baby," I beg, tears streaming down my cheeks, my heart racing, pounding in my ears.

We haven't had any time. We wasted so much. I was stupid and insecure. He was proud and afraid. We haven't had any time and now it may be too late.

"Oh my God," I cry. "I love you so much. Please wake up for me. Please be okay."

Drake manages to pull Beau off Tony, giving Tony enough time to scramble free and get to his feet. Drake holds the dog back by his collar, telling him, "No! Sit! Stop!", but Beau doesn't hear or care.

"Beau, come!" I shout. "Come to Liam!"

The big Ridgeback's attention shifts. He turns his giant head. His intelligent eyes trail to Liam's figure, slumped in my embrace.

"Come, boy," I repeat. "Come to Liam."

He does as he's asked, dropping his head, relaxing his aggressive posture. He comes to Liam, sniffing him, licking his face, tasting Liam's blood. He shoves his massive body against Liam's torso and drops, facing us. His posture is alert, watchful, and above all, deeply concerned. He whines.

Somewhere far off in the distance, I hear the sound of sirens. I know they're for us.

Because I can't do anything else, I lift Liam's hand and place it on Beau's shoulder, hoping Liam can feel the familiar soft fur of his best friend's coat.

"Beau's here," I whisper in Liam's ear. "I'm here. We love you."

Drake puts Tony back down on the floor, crouching painfully on his knees, his hands bound behind him. He stares at me – perhaps at Liam too – his expression wracked with real pain.

"What's he got that I don't have?" he asks, his question – I presume – aimed at me.

I can't imagine what Tony expects to hear. The question is easy enough to answer, so I do.

"Decency," I respond through rage and tears. My voice is hoarse, my throat heavy. "He's the best man I've ever known. You're not fit to clean his boots."

Tony stares at me for a moment, his expression confounded, as if he doesn't grasp the meaning of the words I've used. Finally, he nods, accepting my answer. He smirks sadly, almost with resignation. "I never learned how to be decent," he says. "I learned everything else but that trying to impress you."

The sirens come closer. In another few moments they'll be at my door.

Drake hauls Tony to his feet, dragging him outside to meet the police. I hug Liam tighter, listening to the shallow rattle of his breathing. I notice just then, that his eyelids flutter ever so slightly.

A moment later, a team of EMTs appear. They flood into the room with the assistant police chief, Carrie Jackson. One of them puts a hand on my shoulder. "Hey, it's Grayson, right?"

I look up at an angular, chiseled face. His eyes are deep and kind. "Yeah."

"I'm Jack Chance. I'll be making sure that your friend is okay."

"Liam. His name is Liam."

"Okay. We'll be taken care of Liam."

"I know you," I say, tears forming in my eyes. "You're Dillon's husband."

"Yeah, I am. I hate to have to ask you this, but we're going to need Liam flat on the floor. Okay?"

I nod, resigned. I don't know Dillon or Jack well, but I know of them through Elias, Nikki, and Gil. Abingdon's gay elite were a good many years ahead of me at Jackson Academy. But they know me. And we're here for each other—whatever we need.

The team of EMTs lay Liam out flat on the floor, take his blood pressure, measure his heart rate, and place a small oxygen mask over his nose and mouth. I hear Carrie in the background talking to Drake; I hear her pen as she writes in her notepad.

Jack and his team of EMTs ask me questions whose answers I can only guess at. They press a needle into Liam's vein, attaching an intravenous flow.

"He's dehydrated," Jack says, looking me in the eye. "Eddy is going to get some fluids going. Okay?" The EMT—Eddy—squeezes the saline bag forcing fluid into Liam's veins.

"He was traveling." I hold Liam's hand. His fingers are dry and cold.

"How long has he been out?" Jack asks.

I shake my head. "I don't know. We found him like this. Maybe not long."

His face is bruised with large, red welts just starting to rise on the skin of his cheeks and forehead.

"That guy your friend just took out," he says. "Is that the guy who beat the shit out of Liam?"

I nod. "I think so," I say. "That's why the dog went after him."

All this time I've had my hand wrapped around Liam's. Suddenly I feel him squeeze, *hard*. I look down into his face and I see his expression shift from featureless and flat to a determined grimace. His eyes flutter again, then struggle to open.

"Grayson," he whispers hoarsely. "Where's..." his other hand grips the loose skin and fur on Beau's back. The dog stands up, pressing his nose forward. He nuzzles Liam vigorously. "...Beau? My good boy. My best..."

Once more my heart skips multiple beats, doing somersaults in my chest. *He's awake! He's speaking!*

"Outstanding," Jack says with a grin. "Sir, look at me."

Liam's eyelids open to slits. He struggles, peering up at Jack.

"Do you know where you are?"

Liam answers. His response elicits more questions from the EMT team, each one trying to assess his cognitive function. He seems cogent enough, if a little blurry. Finally, Liam lets go of Beau, reaching a hand up to me, grasping the back of my neck awkwardly. He can't see me, just feel me against him, holding him from behind.

"Grayson," he mumbles again, tears flowing down his bruised cheeks. "I won't leave again. Love you... *so much*. I'm such a fool. Hold me. Don't let go."

"Don't worry, baby," I say, squeezing him hard, nuzzling his blood-stained neck. "I got you. Never letting you out of my sight again."

CHAPTER TWENTY-FOUR

LIAM - MANY WEEKS LATER

*T*he house smells of pumpkin spice, freshly waxed hardwoods, and apple cider. I've been busy while Grayson's been out of town on business. He's coming back tonight and we're entertaining half the town here at the lake house in celebration of the completion of the merger between his company and Nicolai Automotive. He's not quite thirty years old and he says he's retiring. Something tells me that'll last about fifteen minutes. Gray is the type of guy with a million ideas, the type of guy who keeps busy with all of them.

"The caterers are here," Hill says, drying her hands on her apron. "I'll see to them. You head on upstairs and get changed. Grayson will be here soon."

I check my watch. He's due in forty minutes. There's still plenty of time.

I walk outside to greet Kendall Vincent, who's catering, and attending, the party. He's come well-armed with two food trucks, a rolling barbecue smoker, and a team to help set up, then serve our guests throughout the evening. Kendall's handling everything turn-key, from the main meal and hors-d'oeuvres, to the open bars, to the dessert tables. Hill jumps in, directing people, telling them where to pitch tents and set up their prep stations while Kendall and I linger under the shade of the porch.

"Look at this place," Kendall observes, looking around with wide-eyed wonder. "I love everything you've done. I never would have imagined this old place had so much potential."

The renovation has transformed the house, bringing it into this century. It makes a comfortable home for Grayson and me; it's not just a historic old house. I never wanted to live in a museum, and neither does Grayson. I incorporated his very practical, minimal sense of design and my own preference for airy, open spaces and bright colors. With that, we remade this old house into something we both love. The purists might take issue with the fact that we've painted some bright red and cobalt blue accent walls, or that the countertops and floors in the kitchen and baths are copper-trimmed cast concrete, but I don't really care. Grayson and I have made the place our own.

"It's been fun working on it," I admit to Kendall with a shy grin. "I'll give you the tour tonight. I'll probably need to get away from the crowd at some point."

We've invited almost three hundred people: anyone who's anyone, plus all their friends. Grayson didn't want to overlook anybody, so he cast the net wide. He wants this to be our "coming out" party, or something like that. I told him we didn't need to "come out," as everyone in town knows we're a couple. An exceptionally gay couple. He doesn't care. He said he wants to make it official, whatever that means.

"Who's this?" Kendall asks, brightening, his attention drawn to something behind me.

Beau lopes toward us, his tail high, head low. He's looking for ear scratches and words of encouragement. I've been busy all morning and haven't gotten around to taking him out for his usual, midday walk.

"Beau," I reply, dropping, reaching out my hand to scratch his chest, slowing him down.

"Beautiful dog," Kendall observes, dipping into a deep squat so he can be close to Beau. He strokes Beau with both hands, talking to him, easing him with a soft tone.

Beau looks to me for permission to fall into and enjoy the attention. I give him the nod and he instantly relaxes into Kendall's grip, letting his body weight drape languidly against open hands and arms.

"Damn!" Kendall laughs. "You're digging this."

Indeed, he is. Who wouldn't enjoy that kind of physical affection?

"He's a ho," I observe dryly. "He'll roll over for any old pretty face."

Kendall laughs then sends my dog back to me, apologizing that he's got to get to work.

"If I'm going to enjoy this party at all myself, I need to get my crew squared away so they're not driving me crazy all night long."

I'm glad he and Hill are in charge of logistics for this evening. It's a big deal to Grayson that everything goes well. I don't want or need the pressure. I want to enjoy myself. I'm just beginning to learn how to do that and I need the practice.

"See you this evening," I say, letting him go. "Grayson's due any minute. I need to get ready too."

Beau follows me upstairs, staying close. He's jittery, uneasy about all the company on the property. The last time there were so many people here I was laid out on the hall floor, bleeding, beaten unconscious. Between the EMTs and the police, I understand it was everything Grayson and Drake could do to keep Beau from seriously hurting Tony.

He's been on edge ever since, barely letting me out of his sight.

Grayson is almost as clingy. I spent several days in the hospital getting MRIs and X-rays. For awhile it felt like I'd slipped back in time to the old days when I was hurt, but this time – instead of looking at my legs – they were looking at my head. By all accounts, I'm lucky to be alive because Tony Carrara cracked me squarely in the skull with a baseball bat. I guess I have a particularly hard head.

The whole time I was hospitalized, Grayson never left my bedside. He stayed with me for days, until the swelling in my brain went down and the doctors were satisfied there was no permanent damage. I still get occasional headaches, but they're fading.

Turning on the water in the shower, I let it run, streaming over my hand, waiting for it to warm. I think back to how it felt waking up in the hospital, scared and in pain, then seeing Grayson hunched over my bedside, his hands wrapped around mine, head bowed. When he lifted his head and looked up, his eyes were red and brimming with tears.

Nobody ever cried over me before. Nobody ever cared to say a prayer for me. The relieved smile he gave me in that moment solidified the love I already had growing for him. When you know someone loves you *that much,* it's so much easier to love them *that much.*

Grayson's been in New York most of the week, finalizing the deal with Nicolai Automotive and doing press work to help Wall Street embrace it. I've missed him. He's spoiled me. I don't sleep well when I sleep alone. I toss and turn, staring at the ceiling, listening to the house settle, hearing my own heartbeat. I need him beside me, his body heat comforting me, his breath mingling with mine.

I peel off my clothes, dropping them on the floor and climb in the shower once the temperature is right. With the water flowing over me, I stand a long time, reveling in the decadence of endless streams of steaming heat. There was a time when a shower like this was unthinkable. There was a time, not long ago, when I assumed I didn't deserve a hot shower or comfortable bed, much less the love of a partner. I refused to believe that someone as smart, as beautiful, and as successful as Grayson could ever care about me.

He changed all that. He showed me the way forward, out from under the black cloud I'd grow so comfortable with.

"Hey, you," a familiar voice croons.

Opening my eyes, rubbing them against the water and steam, I see a blurry, misty image of Grayson framed in the doorway. Beau stands up on his hind legs, wagging his tail, getting his ear scratched by the intruder.

"Hey, you," I respond, smiling through the splotchy glass of the shower door. "How was the flight?"

"Mercifully short," he replies, smirking, stepping past Beau toward the shower. His hand reaches up, tugging at his tie and collar. "Mind some company?"

The implication and slightly wicked twinkle in his eye tweaks my dick, making me firm.

"Please," I beg, opening the shower door, waiting for Grayson to strip off his nice suit and shirt. He leaves them in a rumpled pile on the tile floor. "Get in here."

"I missed you so damn much," he tells me, kicking off his socks and shorts before stepping into the shower stall with me.

Just that quick we're face to face, belly to belly, and cock to cock, with hot water pouring between us. I slide a hand around the small of his back and another around his shoulder, pulling him close into a tight hug. Grayson leans into me, returning my hug, his hands firm against my broad back.

"The work is done," he breathes against me. "The merger is complete. The markets have accepted it. The news cycle has moved on, and I don't have to go anywhere again anytime soon. I'm so glad to be home."

I'm glad for it too.

"Turn around," I croon, half whispering into his neck. "I want to show you just how happy I am you're finally home."

Grayson grins, pulling away from me slightly. "What'd you have in mind?" he asks.

What I have in mind requires lots of soap and some patience before everything goes according to plan. It's a tight fit with my impatient, hard cock shoved deep inside him, reaching for his tonsils while I reach around, my fist wrapping his length snugly, stroking him in time with each thrust from behind. Grayson whines and simpers, almost crying out from the exquisite pain and pleasure, while I drive into him again and again.

"Come for me," I hiss behind his ear, my teeth nicking the back of his earlobe. "Come for me while I fuck you hard like this."

"Jesus," he huffs, his own hand dropping low, sliding around mine, guiding me on just what to do, which, at the moment, is to slow way down.

"Come in me," he urges me, "Then I want your mouth on me."

I can accommodate that, *with pleasure*.

Liam bears down, flexing his muscles, squeezing me. It sends an electric shock of pulsing pleasure straight up my shaft, vibrating in the pit of my belly, the sensation growing, building until I can't contain it.

"That's it," Grayson encourages. "Come on."

I pump harder, drawing back longer, his walls and muscles gripping me tightly, hanging on. He feels so good, so hot and slick, the soap slipping between us, lubricating every inch.

My balls seize, drawing up tight and close to my body as

molten, liquid heat bursts through, forced up and out. I groan, my fingers digging into Grayson's wet skin. My knees weaken, slamming into the wall between his spread legs.

I flood his cavity with steaming cum, the stuff pouring out between us, washing down our legs in the shower spray.

I'm barely conscious, barely breathing, still trying to remember my name when Grayson turns in my arms, ripping me out of him. He puts his hands on my shoulders, pushing me down.

"On your knees," he insists with an amused grin smeared across his face. He presses me down with all his strength.

The next thing I know I'm kneeling before him, facing his stiff rod that's begging – insisting really – for attention. I don't hesitate taking his length into my mouth, swallowing him deep, using my tongue, lips, and teeth to tease him out. I bring him close, then press him back from the brink again and again.

Grayson's fingers dig into my shoulders, then occasionally frame my face, urging me to speed up, slow slightly, or keep it, "Just like that." His eyes roll back in his head.

I draw it out, teasing him, using my mouth and my tongue to add pressure, then release it. I use my tongue and teeth to torture his balls, employing fingers to stimulate him deep while I suck his cock, bringing him to an exquisite peak.

"Oh... fuck... Liam... I'm... Oh... god..." he cries, his fingers digging into my scalp. In the next second, every muscle in his body stiffens. His hips thrust forward rigidly and his length swells inside my lips.

He comes, exploding, and I swallow every salty, slick drop, reveling in the taste of his pleasure, taking every ounce of it he can give me.

A moment later, Grayson deflates, his pulse slowing and muscles softening. He slips backward, leaning on the tiled shower wall. Then he slides down, his knees failing him. He drops to the floor, slumping beside me.

The water is still steaming hot, splashing against our reddened skin, pinging against the tile floor, and misting against the glass door. We sit, face to face on the shower floor, breathing deeply, catching up with our thoughts, holding hands like a couple of sweethearts.

"I love you," Grayson says, his eyes narrow, his expression as relaxed as I've ever seen it. All the tension he walked in the room with is now long gone. "You've ruined me for anyone else."

God, I hope so.

I squeeze his hand, lifting it, pressing his knuckles to my lips. "Good," I reply. "I don't want you looking at anyone else. Just me."

He regards me carefully, his eyes fixing on mine, penetrating deeply, as if he's trying to peer into my soul.

"Do you love me, Liam?" he asks. His expression tells me he doesn't know for sure.

I have a hard time saying it. I probably haven't said it since the night I woke up bleeding in his arms, after Tony tried to end me. Obviously, I don't say it enough.

"God yes," I tell him, drawing him forward, pulling him into my arms. "I love you. *I do.* I'm sorry I don't say it enough. You're everything to me."

He shakes his head, pushing the wet hair off my forehead, then touching my lips with his while the shower pours water over and between us.

"Say it when you feel it," he says, fingers rising up, circling around the backs of my upper arms, and pressing my triceps. "Say everything you feel. Even if it's not what I want to hear."

Okay? What's he talking about?

"Liam, if I ask you something else, do you promise you'll

give me the truth and not just what you think I want to hear?"

"Yeah," I reply, "I promise. I'll always tell you the truth."

He bows his head, resting his forehead on my shoulder for a second before taking a deep breath and looking up again, his eyes meeting mine with piercing earnestness.

"I want to spend my life with you," he says, his voice halting. "I want to marry you. Do you think that's something you might want to do at some point?"

At some point?

At some point?

I smile, reaching up, lifting his chin. I lean in, giving him a wide mouth, deep, probing kiss, complete with lip bites and a gentle tug of his recovering cock.

"At some point?" I ask, finally breaking our kiss, speaking the words in a whisper onto his wet lips. "In the very near future. The sooner the better, 'cause I want to call you mine always and forever."

Grayson draws back, breaking out in a grin.

"Really?" he asks. "Seriously?"

I nod, leaning in for another nibble.

"Really," I tell him. "I love you *that much*. We're supposed to be together. You keep telling me how smart I am."

"Yeah. You are."

"Well, my brains are definitely telling me that."

* * *

GRAYSON'S SISTER, Melanie, holds up her phone showing him the *Wall Street Journal* headline regarding the company's merger with Nicolai Automotive. Behind her, out in the yard, people dance and socialize, enjoying the swing band playing under a tent at the far end of the lawn by the lake front.

"Ten billion dollars?" she asks, her tone leaden with incredulity. "You're getting ten billion dollars? What in the world are you going to do with that much money?"

Grayson offers an awkward smile. "Actually, my cut is only about six billion," he says, as if that makes a difference.

Mel rolls her eyes. "I'm serious," she says. "What are you going to do with yourself? You've spent every moment of your life since you were eighteen years old nursing that company along. Then you up and sell it? What are you going to do? I can't see you quitting work. It just isn't you."

Grayson reaches out, circling his hand around mine. He smiles at his sister, then he smiles up at me. "We're getting married," he tells her. "That's as far ahead as I've thought about it. I love Liam. We want to spend our lives together. We'll figure it out."

Mel offers a puzzled, but approving smile. "Married?" she repeats. "That's wonderful and I'm happy for you both, but I don't think that's enough to replace the company. What happens after the wedding?"

Grayson shrugs. "I dunno," he admits. "Like I said, we'll figure it out. It's a wedding and then a honeymoon…"

"A wedding?!" a voice nearly shouts, coming up behind us.

We all turn in unison just in time to see Nikki Rippon sauntering up, a huge smile warming his already gorgeous face.

"You're getting married?" he asks, barging between me and Grayson. "Since when and have we picked a date?"

"Since about an hour ago," Grayson tells him. "And no, but soon."

From that moment forward, there's no point even attempting to keep our plans to ourselves. Nikki Rippon alerts the entire town to our news. He's more efficient at spreading a rumor than a soccer mom on Facebook. Within minutes we're inundated with congratulations and offers to help select a venue, plan a menu, and schedule our honeymoon destination. I never realized so many other people could become so invested in another couple's wedding plans, but I guess when there's a billionaire in the wedding party, everyone sees an opportunity to get in on the festivities.

"I vote we fly to Vegas and do it in an Elvis Chapel, *anonymously*," I whisper in Grayson's ear while some woman neither of us knows attempts to sell him on the idea of holding the ceremony at the Martha Washington Inn, a famous old hotel in downtown Abingdon.

Grayson turns and looks at me when I say this, his expression intrigued. He blows off the women talking to him, turning all his attention to me. "Are you serious?" he asks.

I nod. "Way better than turning our moment over to everyone else. People will be trying to sell us everything from China patterns for the reception to side show entertainment. Let's just go to Vegas."

The woman beside Grayson is horrified by my suggestion.

"Oh, I like that idea a lot," he says, eyes bright and smiling. "Let's do that."

And just that easy, we've got a wedding plan.

Grayson's party goes off without a hitch, but by midnight, it's clear that the afterparty – planned and hosted by Nikki Rippon and his husband Fox – is where the real excitement is. Our guests start making their excuses, moving on even before Nikki and Fox take an exit.

I halfway expect Grayson to be annoyed that his friends stole his party's thunder, but he surprises me again with just how down to earth he is.

"I'm glad ours wrapped early," he says. "Now we can go have fun for as long as we want, then come home and go to bed when we want."

If I had my way, we'd be moving toward bedtime now, but Grayson's got other plans.

"Let's go dance," he says. "We don't ever dance enough. Let's go to Nikki's and dance like no one's watching."

I grin, threading my fingers into his. "Okay, baby," I agree. "But only if you let me lead."

"I'd follow you anywhere," Grayson says, circling his hand around my waist, pulling our hips close together. "I'd follow you to the end of time and back, and still keep following."

Something tells me he really would.

We dance together at Nikki's party under the strobes and laser lights of a backyard disco with a DJ spinning house music with a throbbing, hypnotic beat. We dance arm in arm and hand in hand, with abandon and fearless joy, like no one is watching.

Hours later, at home in our bed, we make love with equal abandon, both of us fearless and joyful.

"I can't wait to marry you," I huff in Grayson's ear, nipping the curve of his earlobe from behind, my breath hot on his neck. "I can't wait for you to be all mine."

He leans backward, pressing his head into the curve of my shoulder, his shoulders flexing tight against my chest. "I'm already all yours," he says, his tone breathless from our exertion. His body is tense, tightly flexed, with his hole gripping my hard length like a fist in a silk glove. "I've been all yours since the first time I ever saw you."

"I wish I'd known," I admit, gripping his hips in my hands, pulling his ass firmly against me. "I'm so glad I know now."

We fuck until we cum, crying and howling in one another's embrace as the first rays of dawn's earliest light slice between the chevron gaps in the mountains beyond the lake. We take in heavy breaths, pulling in air, trying to fill our lungs to aid recovery from the expense of hours of love making.

If the rest of our lives are even a pale reflection of this moment, we'll have been truly blessed. Grayson and I love one another, just as we love this life we're building together. There's no telling what we'll be doing in a year, or where we'll do it. One thing is certain however: we'll be together. We were patient, waiting all those years for each other, and it was well worth the wait. We're done being alone now, *always and forever*.

CHAPTER TWENTY-FIVE

GRAYSON

"*L*ove you, baby," Liam breathes against my chest, gritting his teeth, heaving fresh air into his lungs.

Our bodies are welded together at the hip, muscles tensed, every inch of skin dripping with sweat. I could live the rest of my life just like this: held tight inside Liam's intense embrace, our bodies tangled, heartbeats in sync, fingers gripping, palms flexed, mouths seeking, biting, kissing.

If I'd choreographed every single detail, this is how I would have made it turn out.

I was just a kid and I already loved him. I loved him even though he was older, cooler, popular, and so far outside my league he wouldn't have given me the time of day if his life had depended upon it.

I remember eavesdropping on him and another member of the football team. Liam was explaining why he couldn't come out with the rest of the team for a Saturday practice. He had to work for his uncle on an old historical house. He wasn't bitching or complaining. Instead, he told his teammate how much he enjoyed the old houses. He said he liked imagining himself in them, one day maybe owning them. He said it was easy to forget what a shitty life he had and that he had no home of his own if he was able to imagine that, at some point in the future, he'd have a grand old mansion and make it all his own.

So that's how I began. I studied books on residential vernacular architecture from the colonial period to the Gilded Age. I learned about construction and restoration techniques and memorized things I thought would impress him. I also learned about football, strength training, and sports physiology. I even made up special protein shakes for the team.

Yes, I plotted and planned and schemed my way into Liam's heart. I started with old houses and weightlifting, and I didn't stop until he was telling me his secrets. I didn't stop until we were best friends, spending every spare minute together. I didn't even stop after we went off to separate schools and separate lives.

Even while I chased my dream of creating the perfect battery, reinventing the sustainable energy industry, and reinventing myself from an awkward science geek to a smooth, self-starting billionaire, I never once let go of the dream of Liam Gold.

When I found out he was back in Abingdon, down on his luck and drifting, I went back to my old scheming, but on a slightly grander scale.

I bought the old house he admired so much and fantasized about owning. I put the plan together to merge Theos with Nicolai Automotive so I could finally get close to Liam and stay that way.

"Oh, Jesus," he huffs, every muscle in his beautifully chiseled body tensing. His cock – buried deep inside me – swells. "Oh, fu…."

"That's it, baby," I croon against his downy soft ear. "Come in me. Fill me up. Blow me open."

And he does. He comes shaking, trembling, and crying against my skin. His flesh is hot and his fingers dig into me so hard it almost hurts – *almost.*

I didn't get to be a thirty year old billionaire by good luck and good looks. It took effort, scheming, and perfect timing. I paid attention to detail and I always had a plan B, C, and D.

I didn't wind up here, in bed, married to the love of my life because we just happened to accidentally reconnect at Buskerfest. I put all the parts in place, then I waited. I knew our moment would come. When it did, I was ready.

Nothing in life is an accident. Liam and I were meant to be together. I saw to that from the very beginning. I know Liam didn't always love me. It took a lot of effort to get him here. It took patience and cunning, two characteristic I have in abundance. I knew there were things he needed. I organized my life so I could provide them. None of that has been easy, but it's always been worth it.

"Damn, I love you baby," he whispers against me, this time breathless, spent, his body slumped against me like an exhausted cat. "I love you so good it hurts."

"I love you too," I say, lifting my hand, stroking his head, hugging him close. "More than you'll ever really know."

EPILOGUE

$\mathcal{M}$elanie, Grayson's sister, pours a glass of Christmas Eggnog for everyone. Grayson's mom and dad sit back, relaxing on their overstuffed leather couch with their feet up. They earned the respite since they put on a Christmas Eve meal fit for an army, not just Mel, me, and Grayson.

"We'll take some leftovers to the shelter," I observe. "They're having a potluck Christmas dinner tomorrow afternoon and I'm sure they can use all the contributions they can get."

Grayson's mom smiles, nodding. "That'll be nice," she says. "Knowing we helped make Christmas a little better for someone else too."

It's not hard for this family to make things better for a lot of people. Grayson's parents are on the board of every major nonprofit and charity in town. And Grayson set up a foundation after the merger because—as Mel suspected—he ran out of useful things to do with all that money. Giving back to the community that gave him so much felt like a good place to start. His parents oversee finding ways to spend the money in a manner that will do the most good. The Ellis-Gold Foundation funds individual projects of all kinds, sponsors research and studies, and awards loans to nonprofits across the nation. We focus on lifting people up out of economical crises and building a better world, especially for kids. I work with the foundation now, too, coordinating volunteers and leading construction projects for the poorer communities in Abingdon. We can't do everything, but we do as much as we can.

One of the things we do is fund an after school and summer camp for disadvantaged kids. The programs keep them off the streets while teaching them healthy ways to spend their time. They participate in everything from team sports to marathon running. We even have a triathlon team.

I spend a lot of my time coaching the kids, mentoring, and lending an ear. I've learned a lot about life from these children. I've mostly learned that as bad as I thought I had it as a kid in Abingdon growing up in the system, without a family of my own, I actually had it pretty damn good compared to what some kids have to deal with today.

Grayson and I contribute a ton of money to help offset the disadvantages that plague so many local kids. I wish we could fix all the problems, but money doesn't cure every social ill. What most of them need is someone close – like family – who really loves them and knows how to show it. Sadly, that's harder to come by than it should be.

When Grayson and I got married, I knew there would be a lot of extra stuff that would come along with the union. I anticipated things like having to wean him off of depending so much on staff, trouble with the press interfering in our private lives, and basically all the problems that come with being wealthy and famous. What I neglected to anticipate was the wonder of his family and strong network of friends.

Never having much family of my own, and the few

friends I had moving on after my accident, I didn't have the foresight to prepare for what it all meant.

I've learned that Grayson's mom has a capacity for love that's limitless. She took me under her wing and made a second son out of me. She loves me just as if I was her own. Grayson's dad is just as generous, just as supportive, and always happy to indulge me with a conversation about current sports (something Grayson would rather not do).

And then there's Mel, Grayson's sister. Initially she didn't know quite what to make of me, but now she treats me like a rival sibling. We tease one another relentlessly. I let her win at touch football. She lets me win at chess. We dance together until Grayson cuts in, stealing her away from me. Since her husband, Dexter, travels on business so much, leaving her to her own devices much of the time, Mel, Grayson and I are usually a threesome. It may sound strange, but it works out pretty well for all of us.

"You kids lock up on your way out," Grayson's dad says, taking his wife's hand.

They're headed to bed, calling it a night after just one eggnog. The evening is still young.

"We should go to the Tavern," Mel suggests. "They're doing Christmas Karaoke. I heard Nikki Rippon is emceeing it. That'll be a show not to be missed."

"I'm up for it," I observe, glad for an opportunity to see friends. I've been so busy getting the camp kids ready for Christmas, with parties and presents and food for their families for Christmas dinner, I haven't had much time to catch up with anyone else. We haven't even driven around to see all the Christmas decorations yet.

"Okay," Grayson says, but I hear a touch of hesitation in his tone. "Before we go, though, I want to run something past you two."

Mel and I both stop hard. That tone indicates something big is on his mind.

Grayson bites his lip. He looks slightly upset.

"I did something I maybe shouldn't have," he says. "At least not without talking it over with you first, Liam."

Okay, now I'm concerned. He never does anything he shouldn't do. He's the model partner. He even consults me on what brand of shorts to wear. (I like Jockey.)

"One of the social workers I was working with, to make sure the funding distribution is handled correctly at the youth group in Roanoke, talked me into doing something that now I'm kind of freaked out about--especially since she called me about it this afternoon."

Mel and I look at one another. She shrugs. It should be apparent to Grayson that neither of us has a clue what the heck he's going on about. Grayson's never this circumspect. He's never this uncertain either. He plots what to have for breakfast. No decision is accidental or inconsequential.

"What's going on?" I ask.

He cocks his head, a tight mask of doubt marring his otherwise beautiful face.

"There's this kid," he says. "He's in one of the programs we fund. His name is Jayden."

Grayson's been working with the group in Roanoke because they have a science and math club. He mentors about a half-dozen kids in the club, all of whom come from sad family circumstances, including a very special little boy named Jayden Jenner.

"His mom's in jail. No clue who his father is," he says. "He's in foster care. He's eight."

Tears sting my eyes. I know exactly how that feels. I have so been there.

"He's also got an IQ off the charts," Grayson says. "He told me he's reading The Hobbit. His foster parents aren't

214

much on keeping books in the house and he's read his way through his school library's collection. I bought him a bunch of books I thought he'd like. We've been hanging out."

I'm pretty sure I know where he's going with this. I give Gray a rueful smile.

"He's a handful for his foster family. Being the smartest kid at school is tough," Grayson goes on. "They don't really know what to do with him."

"Have you applied to become a foster parent?" Mel asks without emotion of any kind, as if it's just the most natural next question in the progression of this conversation.

Holy shit.

Grayson blinks, clenching his jaw tight. That's his tell for being caught in something he's having a hard time talking about.

Holy shit!

He looks at me, smiling weakly. "That's what I was going to ask." Grayson takes my hand in his. "Applying to be foster parents is the first step on the road to adoption. The woman I spoke to said we could fast-track approval so we could foster Jayden before the school year is out."

"Adopt?"*Adoption? Of a child? An eight year old boy?* Can Grayson see my incredulous demeanor?

"I think that's a beautiful idea," Mel says, smiling. She slides her right hand into her brother's and her left hand into mine, circling tightly.

"Wait," I say. "What? Foster parents? Adoption? You and me?"

Grayson takes a breath. "Before you freak out and say 'no,' at least meet him first. He's a great kid."

Say no? What the hell is he talking about?

"Hon, I'm not going to say 'no,'" I assure him. "I'm just really surprised you didn't bring this up before. You want

215

kids? Really? 'Cause I want kids! I don't want to stop at just one, either."

Grayson's expression shifts. All the doubt and fear evaporates. A wide grin emerges from the stony chill of his concern.

"I do want kids," he states, almost thumping his chest. Suddenly he's excited. Enthusiastic! "We have so much to give, and so much love to share. And Mel and my folks will help!"

"You bet we will!" she says. "That big old house of yours needs a few trouble makers running around in it to keep Beau on his toes!"

Beau looks up from his quiet resting place curled up by the fire. His expression communicates curiosity. He really doesn't know what he's in for.

"Beau, we're getting a kid," I tell him, beaming ridiculously. "Jayden! I can't wait 'til we can meet him." I turn my attention back to Grayson. "When can we meet him?" I ask.

"Tomorrow's Christmas. Can we go see him on Christmas? I've got some toys stashed at the camp just in case another kid turned up, so we wouldn't be caught empty handed."

Grayson nods, his eyes smiling. With his free hand, he reaches forward and takes my hand.

"Yeah. We'll drive to Roanoke in the morning and go see him to give him the good news," he says. "His foster family has already been informed that we might be his new family, but they were waiting to see if we decided to take him before telling Jayden."

That makes sense. "We can get all the forms in today." I grin. "Let's do this."

"I *did* already complete the forms. And I got our background checks pushed through. And I sat down with the social worker—"

"Is there anything left for me to do?" I laugh.

"You just need to sign it."

"Can do." Excitement bubbles inside of me.

"He's a wonderful little boy," Grayson says. "He's so smart. You're going to love him."

"I already do," I say, feeling the mist come to my eyes. "This is the best Christmas I've ever had."

"You guys are enough to make a cynic like me melt into a puddle," Mel states, squeezing our hands. "Good lord! I'm so happy for the two of you – and for Jayden – I could just bawl."

I swing an arm around Mel, pulling her onto my shoulder. "Don't you dare," I tell her, insisting. "There's no crying at Christmas. It's a rule."

It's a rule I already broke. Happy tears flow down my cheeks when I think of all the Christmases yet to come—special holidays I'll get to share with Grayson and our family. We'll make new traditions, decorate a giant tree in the center hall of the house, and spoil the kids rotten with limitless love and cool toys.

Grayson has never made an accidental decision in his entire life. I'll never believe, even for a minute, that he didn't know exactly what he was doing when he completed the paperwork for the foster application. That said, he still manages to make me happy. He thinks he's the originator of all the new ideas in this relationship. Little does he know, I'm the one who suggested the science and math club for the group at Roanoke after I saw Jayden Jenner's test scores. I'm the one who suggested Grayson mentor the group. I'm also the one who sent the social worker to sit in on his coaching sessions with Jayden so she could encourage Grayson to think about the boy's future.

He thinks he's so smart, but smart never out-performs

cunning. It was a long con, just like everyone thought I was running.

It's a good thing we love each other so damn much. Otherwise, our plotting and manipulation might get in the way of this happily ever after life we've schemed together.

ABOUT THE AUTHOR

Tatum West is a writer and lover of MM romance. She grew up queer in a straight world. She's now a mom of two, a dog-mom of one, and she's working hard to raise kids who know that love is love and see the magic and depth of all human interactions. She crochets, crafts, and creates. She's so glad she gets to write for a living and make characters who speak to her soul.

Tatum hails from Virginia and went to camp every summer near Abingdon. The Abingdon of the *Bridge to Abingdon* is a fictionalized version of many small towns, all thrown together and rolled up into one. The men of the town are the ideals created by her heart and mind, all on their paths to true love.

* * *

Look for the rest of my books on Amazon.
The print and kindle editions are all available on my author page.
You can find more information at www.tatumwest.com.

42546326R10136

Made in the USA
Lexington, KY
18 June 2019